A SCREAM IN THE NIGHT

A Scream in the Night

Andrew Hess

Contents

1

Drinna Adams stared at the clock behind the bar. Her fingers drummed on the countertop, anxiously counting down the minutes until her shift ended. It began at four that afternoon, where she waited on tables for hours. There weren't large crowds of people, which made the time go by slower, but the tips were bigger than the bartender for the dayshift made. It was a role she took up during the nightshift.

Thursday nights were busy at the Crowe's Nest. It had a steady stream of patrons flowing into the bar until eleven. Then, the heavy traffic poured through the doors, keeping the place packed until closing. Management loved big turnouts, and so did the bartenders. It made the time go by faster, it was a quicker paced environment, and more people meant more money.

Unfortunately, the increased traffic brought in tougher crowds. Drinna and other female staff members were forced to deal with desperate men, who craved the attention of a female bartender; creepy guys, who believed they had a connection with the women at the bar; and cocky jerks, who thought women would beg to hand over their numbers to them.

Drinna breathed a sigh of relief the moment security ushered the last customer out of the bar. She leaned against the counter, letting exhaustion claim what was left of her energy.

One of the waitresses approached and pulled one of the stools away from the bar. She tugged on a piece of fabric, allowing her blonde hair to fall against her shoulders.

"Rough night?" Jenny asked.

Drinna blew out another deep breath. "Yeah, hopefully this makes up for me feeling wiped out." She took the tips from the jar and began counting it with the rest of the staff.

The man behind the bar slid over to the two women. He was tall, nearly reaching six-two. His towering presence intimidated most men and drew the attention of female customers, but not his co-workers.

"It's been fun watching our girl fending off guys all night." The plastered smile on Akeem's face gave the impression he enjoyed watching the male customers striking out with Drinna. "Tell me; how many guys tried to slip you their number tonight?"

Drinna didn't want to play into Akeem's comment, but the eager look on Jenny's face made her give-in. She pulled a handful of napkins, business cards and scraps of paper from her pocket. Her co-workers smirked as they counted each one.

"I have thirteen just from tonight. That's not including the two I got this afternoon while waiting tables."

Jenny sifted through the pile. She cast away the napkins and pieces of paper, focusing her attention on the business cards. "Were any of them hot?"

"I don't check them out." Drinna brushed the pile into the garbage before plucking the two cards from Jenny's hands. "Besides, I have a man at home, who treats me like a queen."

Akeem flicked his wrist and tapped his gold-plated watch. "Oh, that's right." His tone changed from playful to mocking. "Where is Mr. Wonderful tonight? Shouldn't he be here already to pick you up?"

Drinna let a small sigh escape. "He's out with his friends."

"So, he's *not* giving you a ride home?"

Drinna could almost see the devious thoughts running through Akeem's head. She knew nothing good would come from his mouth.

"His friends were supposed to pick him up from the apartment." Drinna took a rag and wiped down the top of the bar aggressively. "He gave me his car for the night."

She glanced at Akeem to see the little hope in his eyes die. Drinna stood up and retrieved the car keys from her pocket, twirling them around her finger with a satisfying smirk.

"Look at you," Akeem continued in his mocking tone. "You finally graduated to a big girl. You don't need your chauffer to drive you around for once."

Jenny placed a hand on Drinna's arm, preventing her from firing back an insult at their co-worker. "Sweetie, he wishes he could be the man to drive you around all the time."

"Yeah, as long as she took care of me the way she takes care of her man." The smile on Akeem's face was like a window into his mind, displaying his desire to have Drinna.

Both women appeared repulsed by the comment, but only Jenny spoke in reply. "You're disgusting."

"I'm just being real. I'm all about me. I won't mess with a girl unless I get what I want."

"Maybe *that's* why you can't keep a woman for longer than a week." Drinna let out a laugh as she watched her comment wipe the smirk from Akeem's face.

His eyes narrowed at her. She could see Akeem biting the inside of his cheeks. "Let's see who's laughing when your man gets tired of you and kicks your butt to the curb."

Drinna threw her rag into the bucket on the floor. "That will never happen. He loves me too much." She approached Akeem and whispered in his ear. "Plus, I take *really* good care of him."

Akeem nodded. "Okay, but you better holla at me when you decide to trade up for a real man, someone who can really take you to a higher level."

Drinna grabbed his belt and tugged on his pants. Her other hand snatched some ice and threw it down the opening.

"I wouldn't touch *you* with a ten-foot pole."

Akeem jumped back, shaking his pants to get the cubes out "Yeah well, we'll see," he called out as the girls walked towards the kitchen doors. "You'll be begging me give you a ride one of these days."

They pushed through the doors and into the brightly lit room filled with pots, pans, and stainless-steel appliances.

"I can't believe him." Jenny slammed her hand on the countertop, causing Drinna to take a step back. "Does he really think you would walk away from a great guy, a real man, someone with a steady job who knows how to treat a lady right, just to be with a creep like Akeem?"

Drinna eyed her co-worker suspiciously. "I don't know why you're getting so worked up over it. This isn't the first time he's made those kinds of comments."

Jenny took a seat on the counter she had previously slammed her hand on. "Akeem is just as bad as the men who come here to hit on us. They act like they really have a shot with me." She took a deep breath and looked at Drinna. "I don't know how you put up with it every day."

It was one of the reasons why Drinna preferred to be a bartender over her other role as a waitress. It was easier to keep the men at an arm's length.

"I just keep thinking; I have less than two weeks left in this place before I'm done." Drinna couldn't contain her smile as she confessed something she had been hiding from her co-worker.

"Wait, you *actually* put in your notice?"

Drinna nodded, her lips grew wider as the smirk spread across her face. "We leave for Tennessee in less than a month."

"That's great news." There was a level of annoyance found in Jenny's voice. "Are you getting out of the bar industry all together?"

"That's the plan," Drinna replied. Her head tilted up as if she were imagining the life she wanted to have with her boyfriend. "We have enough saved up to make the move and start over. Plus, Danny is transferring his job and working remotely." She walked towards the computer and clocked out with Jenny following closely behind. "He made sure we had steady income while I look for a new career."

Jenny punched out from her shift and briskly walked with Drinna to the backdoor. "That sounds…. amazing. Can I come too?"

Drinna laughed off the question as she exited the building. "I'll see you tomorrow." Her flats created a small air pocket, letting out a noise with every step she took towards her car. The overwhelming exhaustion took hold of her body as she opened the door and plopped into the driver's seat. The key slid into the ignition. Her fingers turned it slowly, but nothing happened. "No, come on; don't do this to me."

She continued to crank the starter, but the car refused to turn over. The only sound she heard was a low clicking noise coming from the steering wheel. Drinna slammed her hands in frustration as tears pooled around her eyes.

This is not what I needed right now.

She sat back in the chair and closed her eyes as a droplet of water cascaded down her face. She was about to reach for her cell to call Danny, but a knock on the window startled her. She opened her eyes and noticed a co-worker standing there staring at her. She opened the door just enough to see what he wanted.

Drinna recognized him as one of the cooks. "Is everything okay?"

"No," she cried. "My car won't start."

He looked around nervously and took a deep breath. "I can give you a ride home, if you want."

Drinna thought back to the comments Akeem made earlier. She didn't think the cook was that kind of guy, but rumors were notoriously spread throughout the bar, and she wasn't going to be one of them.

"Thank you, but I can't leave my boyfriend's car here. He would kill me." She started to close the door but heard her co-worker propose another solution.

"It's probably a dead battery. If you give me a few minutes, I can bring my car over and give you a jump."

"That would be great; thank you."

"Sure, I'll be right back." The cook walked around the corner, disappearing from sight.

Drinna pulled the lever and opened the hood of the car, waiting for her co-worker to return. She had hoped it would be something simple, like a dead battery. Then, she could get the car home, and let her boyfriend deal with it in the morning.

There were footsteps coming from the building. She turned but couldn't see anyone. It was too dark to see anything unless they stood near the outside lights. Drinna continued to scan the area, hoping to see the silhouette of a cat or a dog, something that wouldn't freak her out.

"Hello, is anyone there?" she called out.

There was no reply. Drinna glanced back to put the hood down. A sense of foreboding washed through her and her only thought was to return to the bar. Before she could follow through, something hit her in the back of the head. Drinna dropped to the ground, clutching the wound. The pain was so intense, her eyes closed, but not before she felt someone rip her purse off her arm.

On the edge of her consciousness, she felt a warm pool forming around her. She could hear the sound of a car screeching to a halt.

"Help," a man called out loudly. "Help! Please, someone call an ambulance."

2

—————————————

C**hapter 2**

The studio was quiet when I walked through the doors. Employees were slow to trickle into the building, especially on Monday mornings, like today. No one wanted the weekend to end. Unfortunately, we needed to punch the timecards if we expected to have money deposited in our accounts come every Friday.

It was dreadful to work Mondays. Top stories were weather, traffic delays, and any major headlines pulled from the weekend. Usually, there was nothing new and exciting, nothing until today.

My station manager, Ben, sent over my assignment last night through email. I was to do a follow up on a story about new mandates in the city of Atlanta I wasn't looking forward to talking politics, first thing in the morning. Knowing what was coming caused me to slowly walk to my cubical. I sat down, feeling a buzz in the room, one which told me there was a story of interest waiting for me to jump on.

"Serena, I need you to grab Alicia and head out to Decatur." There was a look of worry on Ben's face, almost as if he didn't want to send me to the new location.

"What's going on?"

He blew out a deep breath. "There's an active shooter on the loose. We need a team to get over there and cover the story." He held onto a sheet of paper.

Sure, send two women to a crime scene at four in the morning, where the shooter is still at large.

7

I was accustomed to hearing reports of shootings in Dekalb County. For a month, it seemed like there was one every day. The time of the occurrence was puzzling. They typically happened at ten or eleven at night. The latest reported had an incident occur at two in the morning. I could only assume the person had evaded police for hours and was still on the run.

"Sure, Ben; we'll grab our stuff and go." I attempted to take the paper from his hands, but his grip was tight, and he refused to let go.

"I need you to promise to be extremely careful."

"Of course I will."

His concern for my safety was endearing but unnecessary. I had been given risky assignments on a regular basis. My reputation around the station told of my history of volunteering to cover thrilling stories, big crime scene investigations, or anything containing a hint of danger.

Chalk it up to my fascination for solving mysteries and puzzles. I grew up on detective novels. The story itself was intriguing, but I was too consumed with figuring out who was behind the crime before the author gave away the ending. As a I grew older, I spent my time watching real life murder cases and documentaries on any network they appeared on. I was drawn to them like a moth to a flame,

Maybe that's why I was smitten with my husband, Colton. He had been a deputy at the time, but just the thought of him protecting the streets drove me to bug him about his job. He remained tight-lipped over anything pertaining to his work. I had hoped it would have changed when he took over as sheriff. Maybe then, he would have shared some of the great stories from his past. Those were sealed up inside his internal safe, never to be revealed.

Serena, I can't speak about an ongoing investigation.

That was his excuse every time I tried to ask him about his day. So, I had to use my career to get the information I desired, even if that meant standing on the sidelines of an active shooter investigation.

"What are you waiting for, Serena? You need to get going." Ben snapped me out of my daydream and sent me on my way to my next thrilling story.

Excitement coursed through my veins as I grabbed my hat and jacket, with the station logo plastered across the front, and rushed off to meet Alicia. I slipped my blonde hair through the back of the cap, holding my ponytail in place as I rounded the corner. I raced to the loading area, finding my photographer with the van doors open. I couldn't contain my happiness. My smile must have been ear-to-ear as I approached my friend and co-worker.

Alicia glanced up from the case she picked up. Her glasses slid down to the tip of her nose as she stated at me.

"What's gotten you in such a great mood?"

"Ben changed our assignment. We need to hurry to Decatur."

Alicia shoved the case into the back of the van and fixed her glasses. She turned back with a look of confusion. "What are we covering?"

"There's an active shooter situation. Police are on the scene, and the suspect is still on the run. If we get there fast enough, we might *actually* catch them arresting the guy."

"Great," Alicia replied sarcastically. "That's just how I wanted to start the work week."

The assignment was perfect for me, but it was not fit for Alicia. She preferred to live her life safer, something less dangerous. I knew this would require some convincing.

"It won't be as bad as you think."

"Serena, there's a man out there, running around shooting people, and police don't have him in custody. This is probably the most dangerous assignment we've been given."

"The police won't let us get anywhere close to the action." I knew the cops would ensure the safety of everyone nearby. They always set up a perimeter around the crime scene and kept onlookers and reporters far from the area. "Trust me; you have nothing to worry about."

"I just don't know why we keep getting these kinds of assignments. Just last week we had to cover the story of the body of a girl found outside of the bar where she worked."

That was a rough story to cover. Drinna Adams worked at the Crowe's Nest, and was found bludgeoned to death, minutes after finishing her shift. Alicia and I had been tasked with interviewing Drinna's co-workers, who were all visibly devastated by their loss. My heart broke for them, but my mind was busy piecing together everything they said in an attempt to uncover what happened.

I decided to use another method to calm Alicia. "Let's make a quick stop at Dunkin before we go."

She stared at me in disbelief. "Are you sure? Won't we miss all the action of your active shooter story?"

There was a good chance of losing out on the best shots of the crime, but it wouldn't mean anything to me if Alicia was freaking out while we worked. Her friendship was more important to me than some story.

"Hey, you know I can't start my day without my coffee." I grabbed Alicia by the arm and directed her to the driver's side door. "Come on; they probably have our order waiting for us."

We visited the same coffee shop and saw the same cashier every morning. Kevin knew our drinks by heart and began working on them the moment he saw our van pull into the parking lot. Of course, I was right.

"Good morning, ladies." The door had barely open before Kevin had two cups in his hand, ready to go. "I have a large mocha latte with a turbo shot, and I have a large caramel macchiato. Is there anything else I can get you this morning?"

I was starving, and I knew we would be out covering the story for the next few hours. We put in an order of fifty munchkins, figuring that should hold us for the rest of the morning. Before I could reach for my wallet, Alicia had her phone out and paid.

"That was for last week."

I wasn't about to argue. Free food and coffee were the perfect way to start the day before heading to a crime scene.

I held up my latte in a salute, thanking Alicia. I glanced at my cell and tried my best to look nervous. "We have to get going or Ben will chew us out."

I grew anxious to get to the crime scene. Yes, Ben would have been mad at us if we missed something big, but I was the one who wanted to get the best shot possible. Our pit stop was designed to relieve some of Alicia's anxiety, but I was hoping it was just enough time for the police to apprehend the suspect, so we could get the video of the shooter being placed in the back of a squad car.

It took us twenty-minutes to arrive, finding news vans parked blocks away from the address we were given. Reporters and camera people were setup and ready to go live.

I walked up to a familiar face from a different news company. "Have the police provided any updates?"

"They caught the suspect fifteen minutes ago." I stood on my tip-toes, hoping to catch a glimpse of the police. "Don't bother, they already took him away for booking."

Great, the coffee cost us the shot.

The time on my cell told me there was only a few minutes left before the morning news began. I collected some quick information about the situation before rushing back to the van to help Alicia set up.

"They're calling us," Alicia stated.

"I'm ready; let's go."

The light on the camera shined brightly in the early morning as I stood far from the yellow crime scene tape. The in-studio team just began talking about the story as we went live.

"Police have arrested a twenty-four-year-old man after fatally shooting two men at a bar. Sources claim the suspect had been seen arguing with another man moments before he had been told to leave. Less than a minute later, gunshots erupted inside of the bar, killing a bouncer and another man, who has yet to be identified. The shooter fled the scene of the crime and evaded police for nearly three hours before surrendering to the police."

There wasn't much else to report. The information scraped together was just enough to alert viewers of the incident and the area to avoid. I sent it back to the studio just as the bright light faded from the camera.

Time to get some real facts about the case.

I spent the next ten minutes talking to other reporters to see what they knew. There was no confirmation of the argument, no one knew who the shooter had fought with or why they fired their gun. I made it back in time for our next live shot, where I reported the same information from my previous on-camera moment.

"Come with me," I told Alicia.

I approached the crime scene tape, making my way through the sea of reporters until I located an officer. I used my husband's name to get them to open up a little more to me. I was able to get one of them on camera, telling their account of what transpired. It wasn't much, but it was more than what I had during my last two live shots.

I continued my coverage throughout the morning news broadcast. I continued talking to potential witnesses, another officer, and creating sound bites to be used throughout the day.

The shooting remained one of the top stories, which meant we were on camera every half hour, and in some instances, we were on twice. Once the morning news ended, we were required to stick around a little while longer for brief breaks in the morning show, where headline stories were mentioned.

Alicia and I walked back to the van during the small gaps, sipping on our coffees, which were now cold, and discussed our upcoming plans.

"Are you guys ready for Halloween?" Alicia asked.

"Of course," I replied. "Izzy is so excited to go trick-or-treating with Kimmy. It's all she's been talking about for the last two weeks."

"It's been the same at our house." Alicia took a long gulp from her cup before turning to face me. "Are we supposed to get dressed up too?"

"Absolutely," I said with enthusiasm. "It's our job to embarrass our kids by looking as ridiculous as possible."

Alicia shot me a dirty look. She had a habit of saying or doing something her kids were very embarrassed by. One of my favorite moments happened when Alicia slipped and fell on the grass while trying to kick the soccer ball to her daughter.

"So, what are you getting dressed up as this year?"

"I'm grabbing a megaphone and my school sweatshirt. This way, I can be a loud, obnoxious coach."

"How is that any different than you are sitting at home yelling at the T.V. during hockey and football season?"

"This time, I'll have a megaphone." I glanced down at my watch letting out a small gasp. "We're on again in five minutes. Let's go."

3

C **hapter 3**
We filmed additional segments, sound bites, and recorded full interviews with anyone still at the crime scene. I didn't get the footage I wanted but I was sure to give production enough to air all day and night.

We were done by eleven and returned to the station. Alicia dropped off her equipment while I dropped off the recordings to the editing room. I worked with the team to put together several usable clips for the afternoon and evening shows.

"You're all set," the editor said.

Great, I get to slack off for the rest of the day.

There was plenty of time before my shift ended. I roamed the station visiting colleagues, said hello to people I hadn't seen in a while, and harassed the morning show team as they tried to leave for the day. It took an hour off my remaining time. I spent the last bit at my desk, checking emails and following up on a few things regarding past stories I had covered.

One o'clock, time to go.

It was bittersweet. I was free from work but there was no time to relax. I was headed home to begin my second job, being a mom to an incredible eight-year-old. Izzy was the perfect little girl. She was extremely smart for her age and had a sassy attitude, just like her mom. We enjoyed our time together. I picked her up every day from school, helped her with her homework, and let her cook dinner with me. My husband usually walked through the door just as we finished preparing the meal.

The clock on the stove told me Colton was running late. I set the burner on low until he returned home. I waited fifteen minutes before grabbing my cell, wondering if I should call him. I pulled up his name from the recent call history. Then, the door slammed against the wall, sounding like someone had broken into the house. The noise caused me to drop the phone onto the counter. My hand reached for a knife before charging around the corner.

Colton leaned against the door as he closed it. Dark circles had formed around his eyes, giving the appearance of a man who hadn't slept in days. His hair was messy and unkempt, unlike his normal slicked back style.

"Hi, honey, I said in an awkward, cheerful manner.

"Were you planning on using that to cut up dinner or me?"

I looked at the knife and laughed nervously. "Well, you scared the heck out of me with that door. How was I supposed to react?"

"Sorry, it's just been a long day."

We both knew there was no point in me asking what happened. Colton was never going to tell me. I only hoped being around his family would be enough to turn his day around.

I walked back to the kitchen and placed the knife back in the butcher block. Colton followed me. His hands gripped my waist as his head lowered to my neck.

"Something smells good." He turned his head and kissed my cheek. He stepped to the side, leaning over the stove. His fingers pinched the handle of the glass top and sniffed the air, as the aroma of a fresh, homemade stew filled his nostrils. "Is dinner almost ready?"

"You have five minutes."

I could have served the food right away, but I wanted to give him some time to settle in, relax, and clean up before sitting down to eat.

"Great, I'm starving." He rubbed his belly in a circular motion like one of those cartoon bears from the eighties and nineties.

Colton took a few steps towards the stairs before changing direction last second. He moved towards the table, pulled out a chair and sat down with his hands on the wooden surface.

He's not changing before eating?

I stirred the pot of stew once more, casting a suspicious glance over my shoulder. I watched Colton tuck a paper towel into the collar of his shirt, like a bib. Then, he placed another over his lap.

"You have time to get dressed." I reached into the cabinet to pull out three bowls. "I'll call you when dinner is ready."

That's when I saw the guilty look, as if Colton had been hiding something. He averted his eyes, looking at the living room rather than at me. His eyebrows were raised, almost as if he expected me to question him. His lips curled into his mouth, signaling he wanted to keep the information to himself but couldn't do it. He was about to tell me something I wasn't going to like.

"If you have something to say, then spit it out." I growled in a low volume, trying my best not to make it sound like I was yelling in front of Izzy.

Colton refused to make eye contact. "I have to be back at work in an hour." He cast a glance in my direction, almost as if he was trying to get a read on my reaction before uttering another word.

I dropped the spoon into the pot, staring at my husband in disbelief. Our night together, as a family, was about to be reduced to one hour, which was not enough time.

"Didn't you just get home from work? Weren't you there, all day?"

He got up from the table and approached. "One of the guys called out sick. We needed someone to fill his spot. Two of the guys already worked doubles this week, another has a newborn to get home to, and one of the guys has his kid's school play tonight. So, I volunteered."

Sheriff Colton Davidson...always riding to everyone's rescue.

It was an admirable trait, something I loved about my husband. He would help out anyone who needed it and give them the shirt off his back. I just wish it wasn't done at the expense of time with his family. There were limitations on how long we had with each other every night. I was first to bed and awake long before anyone else in the house. I arrived at my assignment and began work before Colton's alarm went off.

"Will you be back before I leave?"

The question needed to be answered immediately. If he planned on working the whole night, then I needed my mother to stay over and watch Izzy.

The silence filled the kitchen. My hand gripped the ladle and poured the stew into a bowl. I watched Colton sit back down at the table. He had the eyes of a hungry wolf, waiting to feast upon his prey. I was sure he would devour the whole thing the moment I placed the bowl in front of him.

He looked up as I approached. "What did you say?"

"What time are you working until?'

"I should be home by one, the latest."

My accompanying sigh went unnoticed. Colton averted his eyes, refusing to look at me. I was sure he didn't want to see the disappointment in my face. Not only was our family time reduced to how long it would take for him to finish dinner, but it also meant the amount of sleep I'd get would be cut in half.

I placed the bowl in front of my husband and watched as he began shoveling the stew into his mouth. In between spoonfuls, he caught up on Izzy's day at school. I tapped two fingers against my wrist, silently applauding his attempt to bond with our daughter. He managed to still get in some quality time with Izzy, despite cutting our night short and returning to work. Of course, she didn't realize this during dinner.

I took my time, enjoying my food, when I heard the chair scrape across the floor. Colton was done eating. He was on the move, taking his bowl to the sink. It signaled our family bonding was over, and he was ready to run out the door at any moment.

He returned to the table and kissed Izzy. "Daddy has to go back to work, sweetie."

I saw the look of disappointment etched on her face with her eyebrows scrunched up and the bottom lip quivering. "What about tuck-in time?"

Colton bent down and took Izzy's hands. "Mommy will be here to handle it tonight." I could see it was tearing him up to leave her because of his job. "I promise to kiss you goodnight when I come home."

He pulled Izzy in for a hug before darting into the downstairs bathroom to wash up. He emerged moments later, ready to keep the streets safe, while I was left with tuck-in time.

I'll admit; it was a nice change of pace. Typically, Colton took care of Izzy's bedtime routine. The early morning alarm stole the precious moments five nights a week. I stepped aside during the other two, making sure I didn't mess up their flow. It had been so long since I'd spent special time reading my daughter a story or lying-in bed with Izzy until she fell asleep in my arms.

"So, what should we do first?" I asked.

"Can we watch a princess movie?"

"You can pick whatever you want, and I'll make us popcorn."

Izzy had seen them all, but she had been obsessed with the sisters, Anna, and Elsa. We watched the second movie until it was time for bed.

"This was the best night," Izzy told me as she climbed under the covers. She patted the spot next to her. "Can you sit with me until I fall asleep?"

She didn't need to ask twice. I grabbed a book and slid under the blanket to read my daughter a story. When we were done, Izzy curled against my body with her head resting on my shoulder. It was the best feeling in the world to cuddle with my baby girl, which made it impossible to slip my arm out the moment she fell asleep. It took a few minutes of carefully maneuvering my body until I was free.

My little angel.

I pulled the sheets tightly around Izzy, tucking her in to make sure she was nice and comfortable. I began to close the door to Izzy's room, smile still on my face, when a scream pierced the air, immediately chasing away the serene moment.

The sound shook me to my core, causing me to run to the window.

It sounded like a woman, someone who was in pain or fearing for their life. I pried open the blinds, searching the empty street for the source. My eyes darted to each house, hoping to see what happened. There were no lights on in any of the homes across the street. No one had run outside, indicating where the scream came from.

Did anyone else hear her?

I listened for it again but was met with silence.

Was that her one and only attempt to call out for help?

I stood, frozen to the spot-staring; watching; waiting for something to happen. Every ounce of my curiosity urged me to go outside and investigate what had happened. I turned to leave the room. The sight of Izzy sleeping soundly in her bed grabbed my attention. There was no way I could go out and leave her behind. I had to do something. I had to help the woman. So, I did the most rational thing possible, I called my husband.

4

Chapter 4

"Serena, I can't really talk right now." His tone reeked of annoyance for bothering him at work. "I'll be home in a few hours."

I wasn't in the mood to be brushed aside. "Just listen to me." My voice carried in an angry whisper, trying desperately not to wake my daughter. "Something happened tonight, and I need you."

"What do you mean? What happened?" Colton sounded less annoyed and more concerned. My vague response had been enough to stop him from rushing me off the phone.

"I had just tucked Izzy in, when I heard a woman scream."

"A scream?" I could picture him shaking his head at me in pure disbelief. "Serena, it could have been anything. Someone could have freaked out over seeing a mouse, a cat, a spider, or a bug. It could have been from a neighbor's T.V. being too loud, or even a woman getting scared after watching a horror movie."

Hearing the list of possibilities forced rational theories into my mind.

Was I jumping to conclusions?

I considered the alternatives, but my reporter instincts only focused on the alternative options, nagging my brain to listen to them.

"You're right, but it also could have been a woman getting attacked, a home invasion, or a neighbor falling down their stairs. Someone could be hurt and need our help."

I prayed Colton took my suggestions serious. I wasn't so sure he would. It wouldn't have been the first time my pleas fell on deaf ears.

He had cast aside my comments and theories many times over the course of our relationship.

"Fine, I'll send someone out to check the area. In the meantime, I want you to stay in the house and keep out of trouble."

Colton's quick turn took me by surprise, but his warning was not unwarranted. There had been many times I let my curiosity get the better of me. Last summer, I had convinced Alicia to help me spy on my new neighbors. I talked her into bringing over her kid's trampoline and set it up in my backyard. It was a small, circular mat with a hot pink border, fit for only one person to jump on at a time. I bounced up and down on that for a half hour to see what the new additions had been up to. I figured it wouldn't make me look like a nosey neighbor. However, it made the most awkward introduction when they witnessed a thirty-five-year-old woman bouncing up and down on a kid's trampoline in the middle of the afternoon.

"Thank you," I finally replied. I felt better knowing someone would be around to check out the scream. "I won't be able to sleep until I know everything is okay." I added the last part to ensure my husband sent someone.

I stood at the window watching the darkness engulf the surrounding houses, until a loud knock on the front door startled me. A sudden urge hit me. I considered running to the safe in my bedroom and retrieving one of Colton's guns. I decided against it but grabbed a baseball bat from the hall closet before cautiously heading down the stairs.

I crept closer to the front door. My heart was pounding rapidly in my chest as my hands gripped the handle of the bat tightly. I leaned against the wall and inched towards the window next to the front door. A wave of relief washed over me as I saw the police car sitting in front of our driveway. I loosened my grip on the weapon, feeling beads of sweat covering my hands. I was still felt the need to be ready, in case it was someone other than a cop standing on my porch. My fingers touched the doorknob and ripped it open.

The deputy took a step back with his right hand on the butt of his gun. I noticed his eyes focused on the bat in my hand.

"Ms. Davidson, the sheriff asked me to come here to check the area. Is everything all right?"

I quickly placed the bat on the floor, feeling utterly ridiculous for brandishing a weapon at the officer. "Yes, thank you. Please, come in." I ushered him into the house and quickly closed the door. "Sorry about the bat. I'm a little on edge tonight."

"Yes, Sheriff Davidson said you heard a woman scream. Can you describe it?"

I closed my eyes and thought back to when I was in Izzy's room. "It sounded like someone was in distress or scared. It was high-pitched, and it made me jump out of my skin." I wanted to tell him it was the kind you hear in a horror movie, but that would only have reinforced Colton's theories.

"Can you show me the area in which it came from?"

"Yes, but we have to be very quiet. My daughter is sleeping, and I don't want to wake her."

I escorted the deputy up the stairs, taking each step slowly to ensure we didn't make a noise. I brought him to the playroom, which was next to Izzy's. The window overlooked the same part of the street where I swore the scream originated.

"Okay, walk me through what happened," he told me.

"I was in the next room, and I just finished tucking my daughter in for the night. She had fallen asleep. I was about to leave when I heard the woman. I ran to the window, but I didn't see anything."

"Are you sure it came from this side of the house?"

"Yes, sir."

"Did you reach out to any of your neighbors to see if they heard anything? Has anyone exited their house in response to the noise?"

"No," I replied. "I haven't seen anyone come out." I knew how it looked. I appeared to be a crazy woman who heard noises that no one else paid attention to. "I called my husband to let him know, and he told me to stay inside. I haven't seen the lights on in any of the homes within my view. I don't know if they are sleeping or if they are out for the night."

The deputy nodded as he jotted down notes on his hand-sized memo pad. He turned and exited the playroom without uttering another word. I followed him as he walked down the hall and down the stairs. He remained silent until we reached the first-floor landing.

"I'm going to do a quick look around the houses in the area to see if I find anything suspicious. If everything checks out, then I'll patrol the neighborhood and circle back periodically to help ease your mind."

This was standard procedure, but I was sure Colton told the deputy to stay there until he got home just to appease me.

"Thank you," I replied while escorting him to the door.

I locked up the house the moment the deputy stepped off the porch. I rushed up the stairs to the playroom. I needed to see if he found anything, and I was the only one available to watch his back.

The deputy cautiously approached the houses across the street. He peered inside the cars in the driveways before walking up to their owner's front doors. I could see him peer inside. I assumed he was checking for any sign of distress or something suspicious. I watched him shake his head, as if he knew I was watching him. Then, he backed away and rounded the corner of the house to check the sides. He stood on his tiptoes, looking through each pane of glass.

Did he see something? What did he find?

"Mommy, what are you doing?" The innocent, sweet sounding voice of my daughter pulled my attention from my watch tower.

"I was just checking on something outside." I knelt down in front of Izzy and grabbed her hands. "Now, what are you doing out of your bed, pretty girl?"

"I had a bad dream."

I bent down to wrap my arms around her. "It's okay. There's nothing here that will hurt you." I stood up and led her by the hand. "Come on; I'll take you back to your room, and you can tell me all about the dream."

We walked next door. A flick of the switch brightened the room. I watched Izzy climb into her bed and pulled the covers up to her chest.

I sat down next to her. "So, what happened?"

"I was on the playground with my friends. The sky got dark. Then, I was all alone. I felt cold. I turned and saw a monster coming after me."

"What kind of monster?" I asked.

"He was big, green, and slimy. He was like ten-feet tall."

"Oh no," I feigned a look of surprise. "Then, what happened?"

"I ran to the school, but the doors were locked. I couldn't get in. I ran to the front doors but tripped and fell. The monster was standing over me, and then I woke up."

I leaned over and hugged Izzy again. "It's okay, baby. It was only a dream. It wasn't real."

I managed to talk her down. It took me about fifteen-minutes before she finally fell back to sleep. It felt good to be there for my daughter when she had a nightmare. Usually, I was getting ready for work or was already out the door before she woke up.

I exited her bedroom and was about to walk down the hall, but my memory decided to pull me back towards the playroom. I crept towards the window, peering through the blinds. The police car still sat in front of the house, but I was unable to see the deputy walking around.

What if something happened to him? Does he need help? Did he find something suspicious?

A loud knock on the door sent my heart racing. I hurried down the stairs to check who was standing on the porch. I must have taken longer than I expected. The deputy stood, tapping his foot with an annoyed expression on his face.

"Sorry, my daughter woke up from a nightmare and I was putting her back to bed. Did you find anything?"

"No," he growled. "There was no one up; nothing out of sorts; nothing suspicious at all. Are you sure a neighbor didn't have their T.V. too loud? The scream could have come from a movie or show they were watching?"

"You sound like my husband."

"Well, he's a pretty smart man."

Suck up.

Maybe there was a chance the officer's theory was correct, but I wasn't willing to admit that to him or to Colton. I was ready to double-down on my suspicion until I was proven wrong.

"Are you still going to patrol the area?"

The deputy closed his eyes and expelled a deep breath filled with anger. "Yes, ma'am," he replied. "I'm going to radio back to the station and let them know."

I was sure Colton would not be happy to hear one of his officers would be sitting around doing nothing all night, thanks to his wife's paranoia.

"Thank you," I replied in a fake, cheerful manner.

I wasn't about to let him off the hook. I wasn't about to rest comfortably until I knew someone was there to guard the house, and to catch the suspect, if there was one.

I offered him some coffee, which he politely declined before walking back towards his car. I closed the door and locked up the house. I returned to the playroom and made sure the officer remained stationed in front of my home. It was the safety net I needed to get ready for bed and go to sleep.

Only three more hours until I wake up for the morning shift.

$$5$$

Three in the morning felt like the loneliest time of the day. My family rested comfortably, while I drove forty minutes to work. The station was a ghost town when I entered. No one seemed to be around. That was a good thing, because I looked like I just rolled out of bed. The description was very accurate. It took forever to fall asleep last night. I had just dozed off when Colton came home from his second shift.

He approached the couch and kissed the top of my head before walking towards the stairs. I lifted my head, feeling the need to explain what happened. The words were on the tip of my tongue, but I decided it was best to keep quiet. I put my head back down on the pillow and drifted off within seconds. The long sleepless night took me into a deep slumber. My three alarms weren't enough to wake me. The fourth and final one caused me to reach over and pick up the cell phone. The time told me I had an hour before my shift began.

I rushed up the stairs, with my heart beating out of my chest as I raced to grab clean clothes to throw on. Luckily, I had a station embroidered long sleeve shirt hanging in my closet next to a pair of jeans, neither needed to be ironed. I was dressed in ten-minutes with my teeth brushed and hair bouncing off my shoulders as I ran out to my car. Somehow, I made it to the station with minutes to spare.

A low gurgling sound came from my stomach, reminding me I left without grabbing food or caffeine. I glanced at the coffee maker in the break room. There was no way I was touching the station brew. It didn't compare to the ones I made it at home or bought from my usual place.

"Serena," Ben called out.

You couldn't give me ten-minutes to get my bearings before giving me my assignment?

I rolled my eyes right after I closed them and let out a brief sigh before responding. "Hi, what's up?"

He blew out a deep breath, as if he were about to deliver bad news to me. "There was a hit and run out in Sandy Springs. I want you to head over there for the morning show."

The early morning broadcast began at four-thirty. I had an hour and half to meet with Alicia, pack up the van, drive to the address, and gather as much information as possible before going live. It wasn't a lot of time in the world of a reporter.

"I'll get right on it," I replied.

He handed me the information before rushing off. I could only assume it was to give someone else an assignment. I turned on my heel and took off in the opposite direction, searching for my photographer.

"Wow, you look like hell," Alicia said the moment she set her eyes on me. "Did you get any sleep last night?"

"No," I growled. "Colton picked up an extra shift because someone called out." I rolled my eyes the moment I said it, feeling like a jerk for being mad at my husband, especially when he was showing his staff that he was no better than them. He did his job by protecting our city, leaving me to take care of our daughter. That thought put a smile on my face. "At least I finally got to put Izzy to bed."

"Did she con you into letting her stay up or something?"

"No, Izzy was an angel. She just wanted me to read her a few stories and to lay with her for a while."

"Then, why do you have a zombie-look about you?"

I checked the mirror and saw how pale my skin was. The dark circles under my eyes had an un-dead appearance to them. I was in such a rush to get out of the house; I had completely forgotten to put on any make-up, not even concealer.

"I heard a noise, which kept me up most of the night."

Alicia looked up sudden curiosity. "What was it?"

I wasn't in the mood to rehash what happened, especially when she was going to side with Colton's theory.

"It was nothing, really," I replied.

Alicia stood there with her arms folded across her chest. "It must have been *something* to have kept you up most of the night." She waited for me to respond but I kept my mouth shut. "Out with it, girl. I need something for my morning entertainment."

Why am I always the center of everyone's comedy hour?

"Okay, fine," I snapped. I finished the story of putting Izzy to bed before hearing the scream. "I ran to the window, hoping to find the source, so I could help her, but there was no one there. I called Colton and made him send one of the deputies to check the neighboring houses. He came back a half hour later telling me there was nothing suspicious to report."

"And you think what?"

"I don't know. Someone could have been hurt, attacked, or had their home broken into."

Alicia shook her head and began putting her equipment into the back of the van. "But the cop said he didn't see anything?"

"No," I replied.

"But you still think something happened?" Alicia glanced back at me while placing the final bag into our vehicle. She had a confused look on her face.

I don't know why, but my gut was telling me something happened near my home. The scream didn't sound like it came from a T.V.

"I'm not crazy."

Alicia opened the driver's side door and jumped inside. "I didn't say you were. What did Colton think?"

"He told me I probably overheard someone watching a movie or a show with their volume really loud. We haven't spoken since I called him." I stared at Alicia who had her eyebrows furrowed as if she were in deep thought. "You think I'm overreacting too?"

"Honestly, I would have made the same call you did. If I hear something creepy or disturbing, I would be doing everything to make sure my family is safe."

That eased my worry a little. "Thanks, Alicia. I needed someone to be on my side for once."

I snatched the spare make-up bag I stashed under the passenger seat of Alicia's van. It had everything I needed to look presentable for T.V. I painted my face with a little bit of bronzer, concealer, eye shadow, and lip gloss. Then, I began to fix my hair, to get rid of the bed-head look.

Alicia drove us to our coffee shop, arriving just as I put the finishing touches on my improved look. We grabbed our order before heading out to Sandy Springs in pursuit of our assignment.

It took an hour to conduct my interviews with the police, pulling together enough information about the victim and the suspect before going live with the morning broadcast. I was sure it would be one of the top stories, aside from anything political. We needed to be prepared to go live within the first ten minutes.

I could hear the anchors speaking, giving the introduction to the story. They mentioned my name. Alicia pointed at me to signal we were live. It was show time.

"I am here on Lake Forrest Drive, where a driver was found on the side of the road. Their vehicle had been struck by another who had been reportedly swerving recklessly behind them. The unknown motorist attempted to pass the victim and collided in an attempt to avoid a head-on collision with another driver. The victim, Jordan Geist, was forced off the road and crashed into a tree."

We cut to footage Alicia and I taped earlier where we interviewed the witness, who re-told the story in his words, adding the suspect did not stop to check on the other motorist.

"Police advised they are looking for a 2017 black Ford pickup truck. Officers advised they do have a partial plate number, but they are not releasing that information at this time. We will update you with more information as becomes available. Reporting from Sandy Springs, I am Serena Davidson."

We cut from the live feed and sat around waiting for the next time we were signaled. I had about a half hour between shots. It was enough time to let thoughts of the night before seep back into my mind. I couldn't help but wonder if I was right or if it was all in my head.

"Do you think I should ask the neighbors if they heard the scream?" I asked Alicia.

"Are you going to obsess over it until you've spoken with everyone in your neighborhood?"

Come on; you should know me better than that.

"Of course I will," I replied.

"If it's going to bother you that much, then you should ask around. But please don't go into *reporter mode* on them."

I knew what Alicia meant. It was when I bombard everyone around me with questions, digging deep into their lives, and stirring up trouble when there was no need for it.

"I'll be on my best behavior," I replied while holding up the Scouts symbol. Of course my other hand had my fingers crossed behind my back.

"Somehow, I don't believe you."

You know me too well.

I was sure something happened last night, and I was willing to do whatever it took to prove it.

6

C<u>hapter 6</u>
We spent hours in Sandy Springs, covering the hit-and-run incident from earlier that morning. There wasn't much to say aside from what the police and the witness told us. It was mostly repeating the same information every time we were told to go live. Eventually, we taped a segment to be used for later. I was laser focused, despite the lack of sleep. The moment the camera was pointed in my direction, I was alert, on point, and ready to deliver the news.

Thoughts of last night crept into my mind the moment Alicia put down her equipment. I pictured the dark, empty street outside Izzy's bedroom. My imagination ran wild, causing my worst fears to surface.

I stood in her room, staring into the night sky. The mystery woman's scream pierced the silence, shaking me to my core. I quickly turned around, finding Izzy's bed empty.

"Where are you?" I called out. There was no response.

Panic ripped through me as I ran down the stairs calling her name. I was met with more un-nerving silence. I could feel the tears forming in my eyes as I frantically searched the house for my daughter. A creaking sound came from the porch, jolting my attention in the direction where I heard the scream.

I ripped open the front door. The houses across the street were distorted, and quickly faded from my view with every step I too until there was nothing but darkness. I continued on, taking steps into the abyss as I searched blindly for my daughter. Another scream begged me to follow its pleas, driving me further into the void until my house disappeared.

33

"Izzy...Izzy, where are you?"

The scream echoed the empty street one more time. It sounded closer. My feet felt heavy but I ran towards the woman's voice, wondering who was calling out for help.

"Hello, is anyone there?"

"Serena...Serena, snap out of it." A hand shook my body, waking me from my daydream. My head turned slightly to see the concerned look on Alicia's face. "Are you okay?"

"Yeah, I guess I dozed off for a minute."

I could see she wasn't buying what I said. Her motherly instinct must have gone off, because she was staring at me the same way I did to my own daughter.

"Are you sure?"

"Yeah, I just need to get some sleep."

"Well, the van is packed up, so we can head back to the station as soon as you're ready."

"Sure, let's go."

My mind kept thinking about the dream for the remainder of the drive. It consumed me until we pulled into the lot. Alicia parked the van and shook my arm to make sure I was awake.

"You've been really quiet," she told me. "We have a few hours before picking up the girls. Do you want to grab lunch before you head home?"

Her question barely registered in my mind. I was too busy thinking back to last night, and what I needed to do to stop myself from obsessing over it.

"Raincheck?" I asked.

I could feel Alicia's eyes glaring at me. I glanced back just in time to catch her. It was as if she was scanning me to somehow uncover a hidden agenda.

"You're up to something."

I put my hands in the air defensively. "Nope, I just plan on sitting on the porch to enjoy some sun before diving into mommy duty."

It wasn't a lie. I had every intention of sitting outside, while the sun pulled me into a warm hug. I just also planned on utilizing that same time to check out my neighbors to ensure there was nothing fishy going on.

"Just…" she paused. I assumed she was trying to find the right way to phrase what she wanted to say. "Please stay out of trouble."

I should have been insulted by her request, but we both knew I was prone to doing something I shouldn't.

"I'll be on my best behavior."

"Somehow, I doubt that."

I lingered around the station for an hour, using the time to catch up with some of my colleagues who had been out in the field or crew who were just coming out of editing. After making my rounds, I decided to head home for the day.

I nearly burst through the front door. Many morning show staff collapsed the moment they entered their house. I had something more important than sleep on my mind. Iran up the stairs, kicking my shoes off the moment I entered my bedroom. I quickly stripped out of my work clothes and made a beeline for a hot shower to wash away the gross feeling of standing outside in the autumn sun. We were still setting above average temperatures in late October, hitting the high seventies every afternoon. My living room would have felt like a sauna if it wasn't for the central AC being on. Yet here I was pulling on a pair of shorts and a bulldog's sweatshirt.

My body craved the comfort of my bed, begging for a few hours of sleep. However, my mind was the one pulling the strings, and it was focused on what happened last night. I went downstairs and put on a new pot of coffee.

You can't have a stakeout without a good cup of Joe.

My hand reached out for the cabinet when the doorbell rang. My head snapped towards the front door. No one came to the house in the middle of the day, unless it was someone delivering a package. I wasn't expecting anything. When the bell rang a second time, I knew the person on the other side of the door wasn't dropping something off.

I slowly took a step back and crept towards the living room. There was a shadow standing behind the frosted glass window. The bell went off a third time. The person was persistent. They weren't going away until I came to the door. Every possible scenario ran through my head, immediately jumping to the worst conclusions.

Was this person trying to break into my house? No, they would have knocked in a window by now, or attempted to pick the lock. Plus, I doubt they would be ringing the bell. But they probably saw my car parked in the driveway and wanted to check if someone was home. Should I grab something heavy just in case they try to push their way in? The baseball bat from last night is in the closet next to the door.

The debate continued as I walked across the living room. I was a few feet from meeting the stranger on my porch. My hand stretched out, almost touching the knob.

Maybe it's a nosey neighbor. After all, I did have a cop car sitting in front of my house for most of the night.

That last idea was something to consider. It was very possible someone from the block saw me come home and was looking for some gossip. If it was, I could turn it around on them and see what they knew about the scream from last night.

"I'm coming," I finally announced. The last few cautious steps had more confidence behind them. I gripped the knob firmly and pulled the door open. "Alicia- what are you doing here?"

Her head was titled down, pointed in the direction of the phone in her right hand. It looked like she was trying to send a text, but my sudden appearance seemed to catch her by surprise. Alicia jumped, almost dropping her cell and the plastic bag dangling from her wrist.

"It's about time you answered the door. I was starting to worry something happened to you.

"Why would you think that?" I stepped aside and let Alicia into my home. I had hoped she waited to respond until after I closed the door.

She stared at me like I asked a stupid question. "You told me what happened last night. You had a mischievous look on your face when we got back to the station. So, I naturally thought you were up to no good." Alicia paused and stared at the guilty expression that must have been on my face. "You promised me you weren't going to stir up any trouble, and we both know that was a lie. So, I came over to make sure you were okay."

"I was just making myself some coffee," I replied. "I wanted to sit outside on the porch for a little bit to clear my mind. You're free to join me, if you'd like." My eyes darted to the bag clinging to Alicia's wrist. I could see there was some sort of pastry box sitting inside. "What's in there?"

Alicia briskly walked to the kitchen and placed the bag on the counter. She removed a small white box before taking off the tape. She pushed the top back revealing a pumpkin pie.

"I figured we could indulge in something sweet before you go off and cause more trouble in your community."

I let out a smile, which indicated Alicia knew me too well. We both had a bad sweet tooth. Fall was prime pumpkin season and my home was already covered in autumn decorations. There were blankets and throw pillows with leaf designs on them strewn across my beige couch. The mantle and end tables had pictures of my family from our trips to the farm. I even had a Christmas tree up for most of the year in support of Treegate. This month had Halloween and fall ornaments proudly on display with orange garland wrapped around the branches. I loved everything about the season, and that included its desserts.

I opened the refrigerator door, pulling out a can of whipped cream and a bottle of coffee creamer with an orange top. The label had a picture of a pumpkin pie displayed.

"I think these will pair with it nicely."

We sat around the kitchen for a few minutes, devouring the pie while sipping on our pumpkin spiced coffee. There was some small talk, mostly discussing the story we covered that morning. Eventually, Alicia moved the conversation back to the same thing plaguing both of our minds.

"So, what exactly happened last night?"

Alicia noted earlier I was prone to getting in trouble, but she loved when I brought her into my craziness. Sweet, innocent Alicia lived vicariously through my stories, but she needed me to lead the charge.

"Come upstairs," I told her while I snatched my mug of coffee.

We traveled up to Izzy's room. The bed was perfectly made. Her toys were put away and stacked neatly in the corner. She was such a good kid. I shuddered to think something happened so close to the house.

My mind pictured last night. The room appeared dark as I stood in the doorway. I thought about the scream, the same one that forced fearful thinking into my mind.

Whatever happened last night; could have been us.

"This is where you heard it?" Alicia asked.

"I tucked my sweet girl in for the night and was about to leave the room." I moved towards the window, peering out the blinds, looking at the houses across the street just as I had done the night before. "The scream sounded like it came from there, but I didn't see any lights on or any movement."

"What about when Colton sent the cop over to check things out?"

I shook my head. "I stood up here for a while and didn't see anything. He checked the cars in the driveways. I saw him looking in the windows of the houses across the street, but he came back saying there was nothing suspicious."

Being there, thinking about the woman's scream, made my chest feel heavy. It was getting harder to breathe. My heart began to beat faster until I turned away. I managed to take deep breath and as I walked out of the room. Despite the lack of evidence, I was certain an incident occurred in my community. I just needed to know which house and who it involved.

Alicia and I went downstairs and hung out on the front porch with our coffees and another slice of pie. I kicked off my flip flops and rested my feet on the rail, letting the sun bathe them in its light. My eyes locked onto two houses across the street, intently staring at them with every piece of food I shoveled into my mouth.

"I need to go over there."

"What are you talking about?" Alicia asked.

"I need to check out those houses myself."

"You told me the deputy already looked into them and didn't see anything last night. Do you really think *you* can find something they couldn't?"

"He was only checking the visible areas through a window at night. No one in their right mind would leave evidence right in front of an open window."

"Then, how are you going to find anything?" Alicia stared at me as if she had answered her own question. "No, you are not breaking into their homes, especially when you have no idea what you're looking for, and no proof a crime really happened."

"I guess you're right."

My admission was temporary. Running into the houses without any proof or evidence wasn't a good idea, especially when there were so many possible homes to investigate. I needed to be sure there was a crime, a victim, and a list of suspects before jumping straight into the fire.

"You're actually agreeing with me?" Alicia sounded surprised.

"Well, I don't need to get arrested and accused of breaking into multiple houses in my neighborhood. If I get busted, then it better be for something I was a hundred percent sure of."

"How about talking things over with your husband? You know; he is the *actual* cop in the family."

"I already know how the conversation will go. It will be a waste of our time. He will stick to his theory of someone having their T.V. too loud. I'll insist it wasn't, and we will argue about it until he walks off and I go to bed angry."

"Serena, *please* just talk to him. He might actually surprise you."

I doubt it.

7

C**hapter 7**
    Alicia and I left the house together to pick the kids up from school. The girls walked side-by-side until they reached us. We said goodbye before Izzy opened the rear, passenger side door and climbed into her seat.

"How was school?" I asked.

"It was fun. I filled up my chart again."

In her school, each kid gets a rewards chart. If they complete the fourteen days with good behavior, they get a special prize. There was a list of things they could potentially earn; a night of no homework; they could move their desk wherever they'd like; or they could trade it in for a toy. There were more options, but those were the most popular ones, according to Izzy. There was also a class chart where they could get something for everyone like a pizza party, a game day, or a half day of free time.

"What are you trading it in for this time?" I asked.

"I want to see if I can add the points to the class chart, so everyone could get something cool."

Yeah, that was my Izzy. She always put her friends, family, or pretty much anyone else before herself. I wasn't built the same way. I would have chosen the night of no homework.

A quick fifteen-minute drive brought us back home. Izzy hurried inside the house, snatching a bag of carrot sticks and a bottle of water from the fridge before setting everything down at the table. Her backpack sat open next to her as Izzy worked on her first assignment. I took the seat next to her to assist when needed.

41

The first half hour was spent answering any questions Izzy had, which seemed to be very few. They were usually pertaining to math or science. She was an ace at social studies and English.

Once she was done with each assignment, she would pass it to me for review. It took me almost as long to check her work as it did for Izzy to do it.

Maybe she should take the no homework night, for my sake.

"Done," she called out.

"That was everything?"

"I just have my reading assignment left." That was something she liked to save for after dinner. It was almost like a pre-bedtime story for her. "What are we cooking tonight?"

"We're making eggplant parmesan and pasta."

Izzy bounced on her heels. It was one of her favorite dishes to make because she loved helping me with the sauce. She raced into the bathroom and washed up and returned, ready to begin the eggplant coating process. Izzy grabbed each piece, dipped them in the flour, then the egg, and finally the breadcrumbs. She handed me the coated pieces to place in the scolding hot, oil-filled frying pan. The finished eggplant lay on a paper towel covered plate to dry them.

After about seven or eight pieces, Izzy dared to sneak one for herself. My head snapped in her direction, seeing her hand hovering over the browned eggplant.

"Caught you," I laughed. We both let out a giggle knowing she dangled her fingers over the pieces, daring me to catch her. "Go ahead; you can have it."

"Thanks, mommy."

We finished the frying process before concentrating on the sauce. It took us about twenty minutes to get a simple version ready. The fried eggplant was placed into a casserole dish, where we dripped the sauce over each piece. Izzy popped up next to me and sprinkled mozzarella and parmesan cheeses all over the top. It was probably the cheesiest eggplant parm I had ever seen.

I opened the oven and shoved the casserole dish inside. "Do you want to choose the pasta for tonight's dinner?"

Izzy nodded excitedly before skipping over to the pantry. She retrieved a box and held up the spaghetti noodles. They were her favorite. She met me at the stove as I lifted the pot of water onto the electric burner.

"Okay, we have to wait for it to boil before pouring the pasta in it." I glanced around and noticed the dishes piling up in the sink with the used frying pan resting on top. "How about you go do your reading assignment while I load the dishwasher?"

I had become lost in thought. The scream in the night continued plaguing my mind. I needed to find out what happened. I needed to investigate my neighbors.

Don't do it, Serena. Listen to Alicia. Ask Colton for help before you do something stupid.

I wanted to run to my husband, but he had a nasty habit of ignoring my theories. They were cast aside quicker than I could explain why I felt a certain way.

This is a police matter, not a Serena investigation.

The wrestling match inside my head yielded a no contest as outside interference caused an abrupt end. The sound of a chair scraping across the floor, ripped me from my thoughts. Izzy climbed on top of it, dropping the contents of the pasta box inside the boiling water. She glanced back at me with a smile on her face before hopping down.

"Thank you, my little helper."

"You're welcome, mommy." Izzy hurried back to the living room and continued her reading.

A little while later, I heard a door slam against the wall. My head snapped in the direction of the sound. The startling noise instantly made me think someone broke into the house. I ran around the corner to see what caused the commotion.

Colton smiled front the front door. "Hey, something smells good."

My heart was beating out of my chest, feeling relieved to see my husband standing there instead of someone else.

I took a deep breath to calm down before looking at him. "I made your favorite, eggplant parm with pasta." I plastered a fake smile on my face to make sure Colton didn't know he scared me. "Izzy picked out the noodles to go with dinner."

"I'm sure whatever she picked is going to be great." He bent down and picked Izzy up into his arms for a big hug. He set her back down and entered the kitchen.

"What's wrong?" he asked.

"Nothing," I innocently replied.

His voice dropped to a whisper. "You don't make my favorite dinner unless something is wrong or you need something. So, tell me; what's going on."

"I just wanted to talk about last night."

One simple sentence was enough to sour his happy mood. Colton gripped my arm and led me towards the door leading to the garage.

I didn't mean right now.

We made sure Izzy couldn't hear us as we closed the door most of the way. I felt Colton's hand leave my arm, but his eyes had an anger to them.

"I thought this was settled last night when I sent one of my deputies to check out the neighbors' houses and to sit outside our front door."

I knew this was just him trying to be big and scary, hoping I would back off before poking around when we both knew I shouldn't. Unfortunately, this was one of those times I refused to let things go.

"I have a gut feeling-"

He put his hands on my shoulders in a loving way, as if a change of tone and sympathetic words would convince me to give up.

"I get it; you were freaked out last night. That's why I sent one of my guys here to check it out. He didn't find anything wrong. There were no reported break-ins, fights, or anything that resembled a crime." He took a deep breath as his voice had become elevated again. Once calm, he continued with his plea. "So, I need you to let it go and promise me you won't try to investigate this on your own. You're not a cop. You are a reporter."

The voice inside my head telling me to rely on my husband was wrong again. Colton was determined to end our discussion on the matter without affording me the opportunity to plead my case. I had a whole argument planned. I was ready to fight him until we came to some sort of compromise, where he would look into my theory a bit more. That wasn't going to happen, which meant it was up to me to provide my husband with some sort of proof. I just didn't know how to obtain it. I didn't know what to look for to warrant an official investigation other than blood or a dead body.

"Mommy, I'm all done with my homework," Izzy called out from the living room.

I started to walk away, but I felt Colton's hand grab my wrist and pulled me back. "Serena, please tell me you'll drop this."

"Sure," I replied with the same fake smile I displayed when he walked through the door. I knew this was the only way to preserve the night. I felt his hand loosen as my arm dropped to my side. "Now, you should go get cleaned up. Dinner will be ready in ten minutes."

I waited for Colton to head upstairs before I ventured into the living room. I sat down to review Izzy's notes and homework assignments one more time to confirm everything was finished.

Dinner was peaceful and normal. I kept my attention on the food and then worried about cleaning up to avoid my husband's suspicion. I spent the next hour with my family watching T.V. in the living room before kissing Izzy goodnight. The alarm for work was already set, and there were only seven hours until I had to be up.

Exhaustion hit me like a ton of bricks when I pulled the covers up to my neck. I barely remembered lying on the bed before I passed out. I had hoped to get enough rest to be much more alert than my previous wake up call, but my mind had other plans.

The scream woke me from my sleep. It was the same one I heard the night before. I turned to my side to wake my husband, finding nothing but smooth, cold sheets. It was as if no one had touched his side of the bed.

"Colton," I called out. There was no response. I pushed the covers aside and reached for my phone. It was missing from the nightstand, making me think I left it downstairs. "Colton, where are you?"

I took cautious steps into the hallway. The house had a shroud of darkness engulfing every inch of space. A flick of the switch provided nothing but an eerie feeling something was wrong.

"Honey, I think the power is out."

Hearing nothing but silence, I was sure trouble had found its way into my home. I wanted to search for my husband, but my daughter was the first person I needed to check on. I crept down the hall towards Izzy's room. The moon was shining brightly through her windows, providing enough light to see the bed. My daughter was sleeping comfortably, undisturbed by my calls for Colton. And then, I heard it again-the woman's scream.

I darted to the window, hoping to find the source. The street below was empty. There were no lights on in any of the houses. It was like déjà vu. This time, I was ready to run out the door in search of the person in trouble. I spun on my heel, but the corner of my eye noticed the bed was empty.

"Izzy, where'd you go?"

Moments before, her bed had been occupied by an angelic little girl, bundled up under her blankets. And now, she was missing.

Another scream pierced the silent house. This time, it was closer, almost right outside my home. I was torn between the desire to find the person who was in trouble and locating my daughter. The choice was obvious.

"Izzy, where are you?"

I stumbled around the darkness searching for her, trying to ignore the screams. They continued playing in my head like a recording set to repeat. There was pain in the woman's voice. It sounded like someone was hurting or slowly killing her.

"Izzy," I called out again. This time, I dropped to my knees to check under the bed. There was nothing but a black emptiness staring back at me. "Please, someone, answer me."

I sat back on my feet, letting the tears stream down my face. The woman's screams intensified the more I tried to push them from my mind. Soon, they were the only sound I heard. Finally, I jumped to my feet and ran down the stairs. The front door was open. A cold breeze infiltrated my home, pushing against me as I tried to escape.

I forced my way onto the porch. The wind stopped. The screams ceased to exist. My eyes scanned the block, searching for Izzy or my husband. There was only one person in plain sight. He stood in the middle of the street. My feet slapped the pavement as I tried to get closer. The identity of the man remained hidden behind the darkness.

"You can't save her," the man's voice called out. "It's too late. You need to let her go."

"Who is she? What did you do to her?" My voice was bold and demanding. Meanwhile, my legs were about to give out from the pure terror racing through my mind.

"You don't want to know." The man's head tilted towards my house. His attention seemed to be focused on Izzy's window. "Don't put your family in danger over this." Without another word, the man turned and walked away. Fog settled in behind him.

I tried to pursue. There were so many questions I needed answers for, and this unknown man happened to be the only person who could provide them. I attempted to take a step but was unable to move. It was as if my feet had been cemented to the ground. I continued to struggle. I needed to move. I needed to go after the shadowy figure. With one last burst of energy, I lunged forward, falling to the pavement as I freed my feet.

That was the moment when I woke. Sweat dripped down my body as I sat up in bed. I turned to my left and saw Colton sleeping soundly next to me. He had been unfazed by my restless night. The nightmare had my heart racing.

There's no way I'm going back to sleep tonight.

My mind had a habit of playing games with me, but this time I was sure there was a woman out there needing help. I seemed to be the only one who heard her scream, or maybe I was the only one who cared.

I climbed out of bed and checked on Izzy. She was right where she was supposed to be. Breathing a sigh of relief, I entered her room and kissed my daughter on the forehead before pulling the covers up across her shoulders. It was too much like the night before, almost like déjà vu. I crossed the room to the window and stared out them again. My eyes searched the night for a suspect, a victim, or a piece of evidence to point me in the right direction. Maybe I was hoping for a neighbor to raise their volume too loud, so it would confirm Colton's theory. At least then, I could go back to sleep and put it all behind me.

I desperately wanted to join my husband in bed, but the glowing green numbers showed I had forty minutes before my alarm was set to go off. It was another sleepless night.

I guess it's time to get ready.

I returned to my room and entered the shower. Water rained down on my head, but it could not drown out my thoughts.

I need to figure this out before I go insane. Maybe I already am.

8

I never went back to sleep. The nightmare had shaken me to my core. I paced every inch of the house, fearing someone would break-in to take my daughter. Every lap began with checking on Izzy. Once I knew she was tucked safely in her bed, I began roaming the rest of the house, checking every window to ensure no one was lurking around outside.

The alarm on my phone pried me away from my obsession. It was time to get ready for work, but I was in no mood to spend the time putting on make-up or doing my hair. I ventured back into my bedroom to grab some clothes. It was another t-shirt, jeans, and station-branded sweatshirt day for me. I kissed Izzy's forehead. I wanted to call out, so I could spend the rest of the night protecting her from the shadowy man from my nightmare.

You're being ridiculous. It was just a dream.

I forced myself to leave the house. I rushed to work, believing I was arriving just in time. It would have been the second day I made it under the wire. My eyes glanced up at the clock. I was fifteen minutes early.

I looked in the mirror and gasped. *Well, I know what I'm doing from now until the start of my shift.*

I retrieved a brush and spare make-up kit from my desk drawer and began working on the frizzled mess my hair had become.

"Are you okay?" Alicia asked the moment she approached my desk. Apparently, my attempt to conceal the night of no sleep was a complete failure. "Don't tell me it happened again."

49

I aggressively rubbed more concealer around my eyes to hide the dark circles. "No," I growled. "But now I hear it every time I close my eyes." I continued to paint on my camera-ready face, hoping our viewers wouldn't be able to notice I walked into work sleep deprived.

"What did Colton have to say about it?"

I turned and stared at Alicia. "He told me to drop it." As if she expected me to tell her anything different. "He is sticking to his deputy's assessment. He didn't find anything suspicious, so he insists there is nothing else to look into."

I could see the smirk on Alicia's face. "We both know you're not going to let this go." She kept staring at me, almost expecting me to reveal my master plan to uncover the truth. "Well-"

I turned my attention towards the small mirror on my desk. My silence was a response louder than any words I could have spoken. After allowing time for Alicia's mind to wander wildly into the unknown, I decided to steer the discussion in another direction.

"Have you seen Ben this morning?" I caught Alicia shake her head uncontrollably, as if she attempted to piece Ben with our previous conversation. "I wanted to see where he was sending us today.

My curiosity had a desire for something fun and exciting. It needed to be fed something dangerous or entertaining to distract me from my late-night obsession. Ben knew I was fearless when it came to delivering a report. It was the reason why I was sent to cover shootings, stabbings, bomb threats, fires, major accidents, and severe weather condition stories.

"I think he's in his office."

Ben's ears must have been ringing. He showed up less than a minute later. His eyes eagerly scanned the cubicles for his staff.

"Serena," he said while approaching my desk.

I tried to contain my excitement, knowing I was about to get my assignment. Most of the field reporters found out by email prior to their arrival. I was one of the few who were told after my arrival, which meant it was breaking news.

"I was just about to come see you," I told him.

"Perfect," he replied. "There's a car accident off of I-285 at exit fifteen. I need you to get down there to help cover the story."

That was it? That was my big story of the day?

All the excitement and anticipation that had welled up inside of me deflated quickly, like the air in an untied balloon.

I know I should have been happy to be sent to the field to report the news. But I covered a shooting and a hit-and-run during my last two shifts. Now, I was being sent to stand on the side of the road to get camera shots on stand-still traffic.

I snatched the paper from Ben and stared him down. He made a haste exit without another word and found another reporter to hand an assignment to. I kept my mouth shut, feeling a rage ready to explode at any moment.

"Come on," Alicia said. "Let's get down to the van."

I power walked out to the parking garage, refusing to speak to anyone on the way. I held my tongue until Alicia and I secluded ourselves in the safety of our vehicle.

"Seriously…an accident…that's what he wants us to cover?"

The outrage spewed from my lips like venom. The intensity in my words had been fueled by my lack of sleep. I needed a good story, and I was saddled with something drawn out and boring as an accident.

"It's a pretty bad accident," Alicia said. I knew it was her attempt to spin our assignment in a more positive light. "There are multiple lanes shutdown on I-28. It's backed up for miles. We might see some entertaining people sitting in traffic."

I ignored Alicia's ploy to turn my way of thinking around. "I don't get why we need to go there. We won't get close enough to show anything good. They have aerial footage of the accident and traffic cameras that can help get the shots they need.

I knew I sounded like a spoiled brat who wasn't getting her way. I prided myself on the stories I covered, and today was when I needed something big. Instead, I was forced to report on an accident which would take me two minutes to discuss on air. The rest of my time would be spent sitting around doing nothing.

Alicia got behind the wheel and drove us towards the accident. We got as close as we could until we were forced to sit in traffic. We were a quarter mile away from the closest exit when we came to a halt.

She turned towards me. "So, do you want to tell me about last night?"

No, not really.

I shuddered to think back on the nightmare. The mere thought sent a chill up and down my spine. Unfortunately, we were stuck, and there was no sign of movement from any cars around us.

I let seconds of hesitation pass before I caved and told Alicia all about my nightmare. Tears filled my eyes as I relived the dream.

"The worst part of it was not being able to find Izzy."

"I could only imagine," she replied. "I would be freaking out if my daughter was missing, even if it *was* only a dream." Alicia grew silent after my story completed. We remained that way until we inched closer to our exit. "Maybe you should talk to Colton again."

"What good will that do?"

"You could tell him about your nightmare. If he knows it's keeping you up at night, he might look into more seriously."

"Come on; we both know Colton. He won't do anything more than what he's already done. If I tell him, he will think I'm being overly paranoid. He'll just tell me to drop the subject *again.*"

My husband was good for sweeping arguments under the rug. His family was notorious for doing the same thing. Any time there was a problem or conflict with his brothers or his parents, they would pretend like nothing happened. Then, they prayed no one brought it up again.

It took us another ten minutes before reaching our exit. Alicia used several side roads to get us closer to the accident. We weren't far from the site of the crash. A half mile of walking allowed us to set up in perfect view of the cars holding up traffic.

Alicia stationed the camera, ensuring our coverage captured the best shots of the accident. I stood off to the side, reporting on the incident every time we went live until traffic cleared up. Once the cars were taken away, Alicia and I were cleared to return to the station.

There were four hours left to my shift, and I had nothing to do. I searched for Ben, hoping he had another story for me to cover.

"Hey, we're back," I called out from his doorway.

"Great work," he replied. "Alicia did a great job. We had the best coverage on that accident." His eyes glanced at something on his desk and then moved them back on me. "Thanks again; I know that wasn't your typical story."

"It was no problem," I lied.

I wanted to tell him never to send us to do that again. It was boring and felt like a waste of time. Alicia and I returned before every other reporter, and I was chomping at the bit to go back out there for something better.

"Do you have anything else you need someone to cover?"

Ben moved a few papers on his desk and reviewed a list. "No, it looks like we're set for right now. If something comes in, I'll send it your way."

I walked away feeling like I was a second-string quarterback sitting on the sidelines. The rest of the team was out there doing their thing, and I was forced to wait for my name to be called.

The first hour was spent wandering the station, talking to friends who were news anchors, crew, directors, and producers. I caught them for a few minutes at a time before they had to either jump on the air or handle some other job-related tasks.

Once everyone went back to work, I sat at my desk and stared at the wall, letting my mind go off into a dreamlike state. The moment it set foot in my home with the night sky as the backdrop, I knew it was trying to torture me with the woman's scream. I shook my head, pushing the thoughts away immediately.

Not while I'm at work.

There was no reason for it to bother me that much. It already affected my sleep and my relationship with my husband. I needed to do something to stop it from happening again. I decided to take out a pen and a pad of paper. It was time to start thinking like an investigator, especially since my husband, the sheriff, wouldn't do anything to help me.

Since I had no victim or evidence of a crime being committed, I needed to put together a list of possible suspects. It wasn't going to be easy. Everyone in my neighborhood was one. I just needed to look into which of them acted suspiciously. I jotted down each of their names on the paper. I had to grab another piece of paper to draw out the block to remember each neighbor to make sure I got everyone.

Brian and Dianne Martin, they live next door on my left. They kept to themselves, but I know she likes to go out drinking a lot. I've seen her come home very intoxicated a few times after a night out with her girlfriends. Brian is more reserved and works late.

Donald and Douglas Pugh live next door on my right. They were the ones I spied on with the trampoline. They were not happy about me prying into their lives, but I get along with them very well now. Donald is a financial consultant. Douglas does interior design. Both make a margarita to die for. Neither of them has a malicious bone in their bodies.

Shawn and Brittany Marx live across from the Pugh family. They work in the party industry. He does photography and his wife plans weddings, baptisms, and any other celebration you could think of. I barely see either of them home unless I'm home on a weekday morning. They typically work nights, which limits the possibility of the scream coming from their house.

Spencer and Renee Michaels live across from the Martins. I didn't know much about Spencer other than he was very tall and muscular. I swore he was a trainer, or at the very least, spent most of his time at the gym working out. Renee works in human resources for trucking company. She was gone most of the day and night.

"Hey, what are you doing?" I glanced up to see Alicia standing next to my desk staring at my drawing. Okay, it was more like a bunch of squares at the top and bottom of the page.

"I'm just killing time until Ben gives me another story to do or I get the green light to go home."

"Yeah, it's been pretty boring for me too." She looked around at the empty cubical area. "Do you want to grab some lunch?"

My stomach growled at the notion. It was ready to go, but I wanted to concentrate on my list of suspects. I had only begun to list the neighbors and had several more to note on the other side of the paper.

"I'll pass. I don't want to miss out if something happens and Ben needs someone to run out for a story."

Alicia raised her eyebrows as if she didn't buy what I told her. "Suit yourself; let me know if you change your mind."

I heard the grumbling from my belly, angrily telling me to go with Alicia. I shook off the objection and went back to work on the list.

An hour later, I had marked off another four houses of possible suspects. It included the biggest gossiper I knew, Whitney Allen. She lived down the block from me, but she had her eyes and ears in every-one's business. She was someone I needed to speak to. I didn't think she was a suspect, but she was the perfect person to help me narrow down the list.

I jumped in the car the moment I was allowed to leave the station. I rushed home with the paper tucked away in my purse. I was eager to people-watch, hoping to get some feeling of guilt or innocence with my neighbors. But it didn't take me long to move one person to the top of my list.

I pulled into the driveway slowly as I watched the man who lived directly across from me, Robert Alexander; remove shovels from the trunk of his car. I watched him from the rearview mirror go back and retrieve buckets, a plastic bag filled with unknown objects, and a large black tarp.

What in the world is he planning to do with all of those supplies?

9

C**hapter 9**

Breathe, Serena. You need to breath.

My eyes were fixated on the rearview mirror, watching Mr. Alexander carrying a pair of shovels to the backyard of his home. He must have seen me pull into the driveway. If I sat there much longer, it would cause him to get suspicious.

You need to get into the house, now!

I watched Mr. Alexander disappear into his backyard. I grabbed my keys and bolted to the front door. I slammed it shut behind me. My body collapsing against it as a new wave of fear threatened to take over my mind.

What was he doing with those shovels?

The only way to know for sure was to spy on my neighbor. I dashed up the stairs and into the playroom. My fingers pried open the blinds, leaving little space for anyone to see me. I had a perfect view of Mr. Alexander as he returned to his car to retrieve more items. There were bottles of cleaner. I was unsure of the type or brand, but one of them looked like a large container of bleach.

I reached for my phone, fumbling with it while keeping an eye on my suspect. I called Alicia immediately.

"Hey, I think I know who did it."

"Did what?" There was nothing but confusion in her voice.

"The scream," I blurted out.

"You found the woman?"

I guess my short bursts desperately needed a little more context. "No, but one of my neighbors just moved to the top of my suspect's list. Someone purchased a whole bunch of supplies, which are perfect for covering up a murder."

"Murder? Don't you think you're jumping to conclusions?"

"I know what I heard the other night, and now someone just bought a tarp, bleach, and shovels. Either the woman is dead, or he's about to kill her and cover it up."

"Serena, please don't do anything stupid."

"Clarify what you mean by *stupid.*"

"Don't go over there; don't mention hearing the woman's scream to your neighbor; and don't go snooping around."

"So, what do you expect me to do?"

"Oh, I don't know; maybe tell you husband. Let him look into your accusations and the investigation."

I rolled my eyes and expelled a deep breath. Colton wasn't about to listen to me. He would think my paranoia was getting the better of me, which would only add more stress to his life.

"Sure, I'll tell him when he gets home from work."

I doubted Alicia would believe me but I wasn't lying. I planned on telling Colton everything when he came home, but not before I did some digging on my own.

"Okay," Alicia replied. I could hear the uneasiness in her voice as she attempted to steer the conversation onto another subject. "Do you want to meet up before picking up the girls from school?"

"No," I said hearing my own voice grow to a higher pitch. "I think I'm going to lay down for a bit and catch up on some sleep." I let out a fake yawn to make the lie more believable.

The call ended a few seconds later. It gave me some silence to consider how to approach Mr. Alexander. I needed something clever to say, but truthfully, I barely had any interactions with him or his wife prior to today. I did know a lot about Ms. Alexander thanks to the neighborhood gossip queens.

Bethany Alexander was a businesswoman who happened to work long hours. No one really knew what she did, but her car was rarely seen during the day. It appeared when most of the neighborhood had gone to bed. I only recognized it from it sitting in their driveway when I left for work early in the morning.

Thoughts of her car broke through the clouds in my mind. I thought back to the last few days. Bethany Alexander's car had not been in its usual place. In fact, the only vehicle spotted in their driveway belonged to Mr. Alexander. That piece of evidence alone made the situation even more suspicious.

Maybe Bethany was the source of the scream.

I had to be careful. There was no way to approach Mr. Alexander about his wife without seeming like I was a nosey neighbor. If he had done something to her or another person, my questions could raise a red flag. But I had no other choice. I was the only one who believed something happened in our neighborhood the other night, which meant it was up to me to find out what happened.

Think, Serena; what does Bethany do for a living? What are her hobbies? What can I possibly say to make Mr. Alexander tell me what he's doing with those supplies, and where his wife has been for the last few days?

I decided to focus on his recent purchase, which gave me an idea. I marched downstairs and hurried across the street just as the trunk of his car closed.

"Mr. Alexander," I called out. His head turned in my direction with a glare. "I noticed you bought some shovels and outdoor supplies. Are you planning on doing some gardening?"

"Why? Are you planning on ratting me out to the HOA about starting one in my fenced in yard?"

His defensiveness was alarming, causing me to take a step back. Maybe I came off a little aggressive. A softer approach might be better.

"No, sir," I replied. "I was just curious. I used to have one and grew several types of fruit and vegetables." It was a blatant lie. I was horrible at gardening and was known to kill every plant I ever had.

"Oh really?"

I must have piqued his curiosity. His eyes stared at me, most likely trying to determine if I was telling the truth. So, I decided to double down by making an offer.

"I'd love to help out or lend you any advice." I was laying it on thick, but I needed to see if he was using those supplies for yard work, gardening, or something mischievous.

"Thanks, but I think I'll be just fine on my own." He turned to walk up towards the front door, but I was not done questioning him yet.

"How's Bethany?"

His head snapped towards me. "Excuse me," he growled. His anger displayed the moment I mentioned his wife's name.

"I haven't seen her in a few days."

"So?"

"I wanted to see if she wanted to meet up for a girl's night out."

There was no way he was going to believe that lie. Bethany and I had never hung out. I doubted she spent any time with anyone outside of her office. I didn't even know if she had any friends, but I was about to make it seem like we were best buddies in a blatant attempt to get any information out of her husband.

"She had to go out of town unexpectedly on business." I could see the anger radiating from his eyes. "I'll let her know you were asking about her." He turned to make a hasty retreat inside his home.

"Do you know when she'll be back?" I was pushing my luck, but I was determined to get something useful from our conversation.

Mr. Alexander's head snapped in my direction. "Why don't you call *her* about it" His hand grasped the handle of the front door and shoved it open violently before slamming it behind him.

It abruptly ended our conversation. He called me on my bluff, effectively dousing my investigation with cold water. Somehow, I managed to get just enough information to present Colton with when he got home. Maybe he would look into my theory.

I retreated back to the house and sat around for the next hour reviewing the conversation with Mr. Alexander. It was still on my mind when I went to the school to pick up Izzy. Alicia was already there waiting for her daughter.

"Well, you're still in one piece," she said. "I'm guessing you followed my advice and stayed away from your neighbor?"

I didn't say a word in reply. I raised my eyebrows before looking back at the school. I wasn't about to get chastised for doing what I felt was the right thing.

"Are you stupid?" Alicia asked. "Why would you go near a possible suspect without any backup?"

"Because I knew you wouldn't go with me," I snapped in reply.

She flinched at my words, as if my statement had been a fist aimed at Alicia's head. She took a step back and kept her eyes trained on the ground. I was sure her mind began to fill with guilt over her inability to stop me from venturing out on my own.

"So, what did you find?"

There's my secret, little, thrill-seeker.

"Well, I know his wife had suddenly left town on business. He also bought brand new shovels and a tarp; like the kind you use to dig a hole and possibly bury a body in."

"Does his wife go on business trips a lot?"

"I barely ever see his wife. It could be possible, but it doesn't explain his latest purchases."

"Maybe he is doing some planting or landscaping in his backyard," Alicia suggested.

These were the same obstacles I knew Colton would present to me as well. At least Alicia would prep me for what I would face later when I discussed it to my husband.

"I tried to engage him in a conversation about it. I even lied and said I was amazing at gardening."

Alicia laughed immediately. "You- good at gardening?"

I shrugged off her comment and continued on. "I offered to help him with some advice or to assist in whatever he had planned."

"What would you have done if he had taken you up on it?"

That was a question I had not taken into consideration. "Well, he turned me down. So, that is irrelevant right now."

"Okay fine," she said while trying to regain her composure. "What's your next move, *Sherlock?*"

"I'll start with your advice, and I will bring it up to Colton. Maybe he can help make sense of it."

"And if *that* doesn't work?"

"Then, I might have to take matters in my own hands again."

"I don't like where that's going." Alicia turned as the doors to the school opened. "Please don't do anything without consulting me first. Let me be your voice of reason, or at least someone who can tell husband where you are when you go missing."

Despite the jokes, Alicia wanted to know what I was doing so she could live vicariously through me. I was sure a part of her wanted to help me, just as long as she didn't get in any kind of trouble.

"Sure, no problem," I replied with a smile as Izzy came running through the doors. She locked eyes on me and hurried over to give me a hug. I turned towards Alicia. "I'll let you know how everything goes tomorrow."

I walked Izzy to the car and took her home. It was the usual routine all over again. Every day felt like it was the same, rinse and repeat. Thankfully, I didn't have to cook. We were having leftovers from last night, which made everything easier on me.

Colton came home a few hours later, just in time for dinner. His tone was upbeat. His eyes were alive and filled with love.

I guess someone had a good day.

"How are my girls today?" he asked.

Izzy let out a little giggle. "Great, daddy; how was your day?"

"Better now that I get to see you." He picked her up and gave her a big hug. He set her back on the couch and turned his attention towards me. "And what about you?"

I felt like his tone was a bit accusatory, but his eyes were still filled with love. "It was a pretty boring day." It wasn't a lie. "Work had me cover an accident for most of my shift. Then, I sat around the station doing nothing."

"Sounds like an eventful day." He nodded as if he was waiting for me to tell him something more. When I didn't give into the silence, he decided to get out before bad news came his way. "I'm going to run up and get changed. I'll be down in a few minutes."

I gave Colton a two-minute head-start before quietly walking up the stairs. I caught him right as his hands turned on the shower.

"Hey, I was hoping we could talk."

He let out a sigh. "I knew there had to be something wrong. What happened this time?"

"I know you told me to drop it-"

"Then, let it go, Serena."

"I just wanted to let you know; Mr. Alexander bought shovels, a tarp, and cleaning supplies."

"So what?" Colton asked in reply.

"So, don't you find that the least bit suspicious?"

"The man is probably doing some gardening." Colton pulled out a towel from the closet and placed it on the hook. "Come to think of it; Halloween is in a few days. He could be setting up his decorations."

"People don't wait until the week of a holiday to decorate the outside of their house."

"I'm just saying there is probably a reasonable explanation other than the crazy accusations going on in your head."

"Really?" I didn't know how to defend myself from his insult. There was no rebuttal. My only move was to throw out another piece of information in hopes of Colton taking some sort of interest. "His wife is also missing."

"Missing?" Colton's head snapped in my direction. "Did he say she was missing?"

"Well, no; not in those words."

I felt his hands take mine and held them tightly. "What words did he use, Serena?"

"He said she unexpectedly had to leave town on business."

"So, you're getting all worked up over a woman who went out of town for work, and her husband who made a few purchases to possibly do some gardening?"

The way he said it, made it sound like I had jumped to conclusions. It was a possibility, but I wasn't willing to admit that.

"Forget it," I growled. "I knew you wouldn't believe me."

He led me to the foot of the bed. "It's not that," he said in a soothing tone. "You're throwing around insinuations without any shred of evidence. There is nothing to suggest anything happened. I haven't received any missing person reports, and I haven't seen anyone else stating they heard a woman screaming."

I kept my head low. Tears began pooling in my eyes. I wasn't sad or crying for being wrong. The anger inside was bubbling to the surface, and my eyes watered from trying to stop me from snapping at my husband.

Before either of us could say another word, my cell phone rang. I saw it was the station and answered it immediately.

"Hi, Serena," the manager said. "Johanna called out for tomorrow and I need someone to fill in as the anchor."

That was his way of telling me I had been chosen to take over for her. It wasn't the first time I had to sit behind the desk and deliver the news. I'm sure it wouldn't be the last time either.

"Sure, I'll be there tomorrow, ready to anchor the broadcast."

"Great, thank you, Serena."

I started to leave the room, but Colton called out for me. "Where are you going?" he asked.

"I need to finish getting dinner ready so I can go to bed early tonight." I was sure Colton didn't know or care how restless my sleep had been for the last couple of nights. But I refused to go on air tomorrow morning looking like I had just rolled out of bed.

I have no time for nightmares tonight.

10

Here we go. Another day; another early morning wake-up. The sun was still asleep, and I doubted I would get to see daylight until my shift was over. Anchoring the morning news didn't allow me time to enjoy sunrise like my field reporting duties. Taking on the role of anchor had its benefits, like discussing more than just one story on camera. Unfortunately, I had to look my best at all times, which meant it took me a lot longer to get ready in the morning.

News anchors, meteorologists, and other on-air personalities had their own offices, where they stashed clothes to change into at the station. Field reporters didn't share the same luxury. We wore whatever we wanted, as long as it was professional looking. Working in the studio made me feel like a fish out of water. I never knew how to dress. It could be an eighty-degree day out and freezing inside the building. This made it harder to choose what to wear and sitting at the big desk meant I needed to put on my fancy clothes.

I slipped on a light-brown skirt with black pumps and paired it with a white long-sleeved shirt. I kept my hair straight but placed it in a ponytail to allow the studio lights to brighten my green eyes. A few layers of make-up completed the look. Right on time and I was camera-ready. Thankfully, I had enough sleep to ensure I made it through the broadcast without passing out at the desk.

Hunger had me begging for food and studio coffee. I rushed off the set to the breakroom. My hand had just grabbed a doughnut when I heard Alicia's voice.

"Hey, are you ditching me for a desk job?"

I ripped a piece of the stale pastry with my teeth. Normally, I wouldn't touch anything left out all morning, but I was desperate.

"They called me last night, right as Colton and I were arguing over my investigative work."

"You *actually* told him?" Alicia placed her hand over her heart for additional dramatic effect.

"Not like it did any good," I replied. "He immediately shut me down, defending a man whom we barely know."

"What did he say?"

I poured a cup of station coffee and stirred my coffee violently, almost spilling some. I narrowly missed getting a brown stain on my white shirt, which made me put down the cup right away.

"He came up with excuses as to why Mr. Alexander would buy shovels and tarps. He told me it could have been for gardening or to decorate for Halloween. What man sets up his home the week of a holiday?"

"Especially for a guy who claims his wife suddenly left town on business." Alicia's statement made me think she was coming around to my way of thinking.

I immediately jumped all over her reply. "So, you agree with me? You think I'm onto something? You think Mr. Alexander could be the culprit?"

Alicia took a step back with her hands raised in defense. "I didn't say any of that." She slowly lowered her arms. "I just don't think a man would put up any decorations unless he's really into the holiday or unless his wife made him do it."

I stared at the break room wall while thinking about the last few Halloweens. I couldn't recall the Alexander home putting up any decorations except for something hanging from the front door or pumpkins on their front steps.

"I don't think they ever do anything for Halloween." The more I thought about it, I realized the Alexanders hardly decorated for any holiday.

Alicia's voice broke my concentration. "Did Colton say anything about the wife suddenly going out of town?"

I shook my head. "He shut that topic down faster than the shovel and tarp thing. I swear; that man never believes a single word I say."

"Maybe it's because you're always so paranoid and suspicious of all your neighbors, even when they don't give any reason for you to think badly of them."

"I'll admit to not having the best track record, but I know something bad happened the other night. I'm sure Mr. Alexander was responsible for it." I glanced at the wall to my left and noticed the time. I had five minutes until I had to be in the studio for my final prep before going on-air. "Hey, I have to run. Can we catch up later?"

I barely heard her agree over the sound of my heels clicking against the floor as I moved quickly towards the studio. I barely wore pumps unless Colton took me someplace special for our date night or if I was asked to anchor the news. Both happened on rare occasions, and usually ended with me falling down at some point.

I entered the studio and was instantly given my mic-pack and earpiece. They set me up in Johanna's spot with notes sitting on the desk and a teleprompter several feet in front of me. The studio lights dimmed, shrouding everything behind the cameras in darkness. I sat next to Roger, the co-anchor for the morning show. He already had a steaming hot cup of coffee set off camera to his right. His face had a smile plastered across it. He was ready for the show, but I was feeling more anxious than I usually did.

"Good morning, Atlanta," he said as the red light signaled, we were live. "I am Roger Hoff."

That was my cue. "And I am Serena Davidson; in for Johanna Gibbons." The teleprompter scrolled through the script quickly as I began to read my part. "We begin our broadcast with breaking news. There is a turned over truck on I-85. Let's send it over to Ryan Herbert with an update on this accident and more on our morning commute."

We ran through the morning weather and traffic before continuing onto the top stories. We were less than ten minutes into the show when Roger spoke of a news story where an amateur video captured a fight on camera. I heard a woman scream on the recording, which sent my mind back to the other night.

I stared into the darkness behind the teleprompter. I needed to know what happened, and I knew Mr. Alexander was the one holding the answers. My impulsive side wanted to jump out of the chair and rush out of the studio, but that would not be beneficial to my career or what I planned to do later that day. Instead, I continued the broadcast as if nothing affected me.

The cameras turned off by seven that morning, allowing me a little more freedom to walk around the station. Roger and I had an alternating schedule, every other half hour, to tell the top stories of the day as the national morning show kicked it to the local side to give a quick update and send it off to the meteorologist for the weather. I spent the first forty minutes sitting at my desk with my heels placed under it. My bare feet rested comfortably in a pair of slippers I had previously tucked away in the bottom drawer of my desk.

The first few minutes were spent winding down from being on-air for two and a half hours straight. Once I settled in at my desk, my mind began to focus on the scream and of course the conversation with Mr. Alexander. I decided to concentrate on the night in question.

Think; what did I see that night?

I closed my eyes and saw myself standing in Izzy's room looking out the window. The street was empty. There wasn't a person in sight. There were no lights on in any of the houses across the street.

Was anyone home?

I tried to think if there were any cars parked in the driveway at Mr. Alexander's house.

Yes, I remember one. The officer looked through the window of the passenger side door before checking on the house. But it wasn't Bethany's car.

She drove a sleek, black, Benz. The one I saw was a silver, four-door. But Mr. Alexander never parks in the driveway.

The car swap meant one of two things. Bethany's car was sitting in the garage where Mr. Alexander usually parked, or her vehicle was missing. That was something I needed to know before charging forward with my investigation. If it was gone, then it could have been used to get rid of the body and make it look like some sort of accident.

I decided to jot the information down on a notepad and continued to let my mind go off on the wild goose chase. The next stop focused on the shovels and supplies. There had to be a reason for him purchasing the items. Colton could have been right, but I felt like they were being used with evil intentions.

No one buys that much bleach and other cleaning products unless they were trying to cover up something.

I made note of the shovels and the supplies. I had to break into the house and check out his backyard to see if I could uncover anything resembling a dead body or crime scene.

Too much time has passed. There would be no evidence of a struggle in the house, and he has had too much time to use the cleaning products to wipe away any DNA or anything that could tell me what happened the other night.

I glanced at the clock on my computer and saw my forty minutes were up. It was time to get back to work. I pulled off the slippers and placed my feet back into the pair of pumps which had become my sworn enemy that day. Every step felt like someone stabbed my heels and ankles.

I sat in the chair and prepared myself for the next live shot. The red light came on and I spouted off the news in a moderately cheerful, yet professional manner. The whole segment lasted less than three minutes. If you included the weather, then it was just under five.

I walked back to my desk and quickly removed the four-inch shoes of sadism. The moment I grabbed the slippers, I heard a familiar voice hurl an insult my way.

"You actually brought those things to work," Alicia called out as she approached my desk.

"What's wrong with them?"

"They look like you killed two Muppets and are wearing their bodies as your shoes."

"They're comfortable."

"I'm sure to tell Fozzy and Grover's friends their deaths were in support of your comfort and fashion."

"Those were two totally different shows."

"Are you seriously trying to change the subject with a technicality?"

I let out a smile and continued on with my plan. "So, how did you like your new partner in crime?"

"Jasmin wasn't too bad, but she is anti-coffee."

"She's going to regret that if she stays on the morning shift."

Alicia rested her butt on the edge of my desk. Her eyes gravitated towards my notepad. "What's that?"

My failed attempt to hide it, only encouraged Alicia to lunge forward, wrestling it from my grip. Her eyes read my scribble. There was no way to lie my way out of the truth.

"I was making a list of things to check out around my neighbor's house. There may be a chance to prove he did something to his wife, even if we don't have a body and no one has reported her missing."

"You really need a hobby."

"No, I need to figure out what happened so I can actually get some sleep at night." I watched Alicia stare at the list a little longer. "Is your offer to keep me out of trouble still good?"

She let the notepad slip from her hand onto the desk. Her eyes were wide with fear. "What do you mean?"

"I need a lookout while I investigate Mr. Alexander's yard and garage." I was planning to do it with or without her help.

"Are you nuts?" Alicia's outburst forced me to shush her immediately. She lowered her voice. "You can't go around breaking into someone's home."

"I'm not; I just want to snoop around to see if his wife's car is parked in the garage, and to see what he's doing with the supplies he purchased yesterday."

"You're going to get shot or arrested."

"Not if you're my lookout. If he comes home, then you can call or text me. I can hop the fence and get out of there before anyone sees me."

I let my proposition hang in the open for Alicia to consider. Before she could give me an answer, Ben walked over to us.

"Serena, can I have a word with you?" He led me away from Alicia. His face appeared troubled. "Johanna is going to be out for the next few days. Since you did a great job this morning, I would like for you to be her fill-in until she comes back."

This was not what I wanted, but I was a team player. "Sure, I'd be happy to stand in for her."

"Great, I'll see you tomorrow morning then."

I walked back over to my desk, where Alicia was still looking like she was wrestling with my request.

"What did Ben want?"

"He's having me anchor for the next few days, which means you're flying solo until I'm allowed back in the field." I took a deep breath and decided to ask one final time. "So, are you in or out?"

11

hapter 11

Adrenaline coursed through my veins as I drove home. I couldn't wait to ditch the demonic dress shoes for something more comfortable. They were off the moment I burst through the front door. I raced up to my bedroom and threw them in the closet. I imagined it was a giant trash bin after the hell they put my feet through today. The rest of my work attire was removed quickly in favor of the black sweatpants and matching sweatshirt I pulled from the dresser drawers.

The doorbell rang moments later, signaling my cohort had arrived. Alicia stood on the porch with a backpack slung over her shoulder.

"What took you so long?" I asked.

"Like you really knew I was coming over here to help you?"

Yes, yes, I did. I knew it the moment I mentioned what I planned to do.

"I had hoped you would want to make sure your best friend didn't end up becoming a victim."

She dropped the bag on the floor. "I already have reservations about this; don't make me call your husband and tell him what you're planning to do."

As much as Alicia threatened to involve Colton, she never would do it. We both knew it would be a violation of our trust, not to mention it would cause issues in my marriage.

"Okay, but if you're going to help me, then I think you need to change so no one can give your description."

"Wait, I'm going in there too?"

"Of course," I replied. "I need someone to watch my back."

"B-b-but I thought you just needed me to be the lookout."

I glanced down at the bag on the floor. "Then, what's in there?"

I had a feeling it was a change of clothes. Before she could reach down to pick it up, I made a dash and grabbed it. I pulled out a pair of black pants, a matching t-shirt, and a ski mask. That one had me puzzled.

How did she find a ski mask in Georgia when we rarely ever get snow? Plus, fall just began. She had to have tipped off the cashier that she was up to no good.

"So, if you weren't going to join me, then why bring all this stuff?" I inquired while twirling the mask around on my finger.

"I-I figured you might need it." Her stammering really showed her inability to lie.

"Tell the truth," I encouraged.

"Fine, I figured you might try to convince me to go with you, and I wanted to be prepared. This way, I could change before we got caught."

I appreciated her desire to be prepared, but there was no way I was getting her trouble over my paranoia.

"It's fine; you can stay here and be the lookout in case Mr. Alexander comes home." I walked to the cabinet and pulled out a portable police scanner. "Keep this on. You can monitor it to see if a neighbor tries to call 9-1-1 about an intruder."

Alicia's hand shook as it took the scanner. "You're really going through with this?"

It was her last ditched effort to talk some sense into me or maybe she was silently praying I would change my mind and cancel the plan.

"I need to do it. I have to know if something happened to Bethany Alexander or someone else."

I stuffed Alicia's clothes back into the bag but kept the ski mask. It was the only missing piece to my outfit. I tucked my blonde hair under it as I pulled the material over my forehead.

"Wish me luck," I told her.

I stuck my head outside the door, checking to see if the coast was clear. There was no one around. It was the perfect time to make my move. I darted across the street to the Alexander house. I wanted to peek inside the garage first, knowing it could contain the first piece of damning evidence. I figured it would be the easiest spot to check without being seen. Unfortunately, that was not the case.

There were only three small windows sitting at eye level. I couldn't see anything through those squares. It was complete darkness inside the garage. I couldn't even make out an outline of any objects, including a car.

They must be tinted. Maybe he did something to the windows to make sure no one sees inside.

My mind was making it out to be more suspicious than reality. I mean; who would want to give a stranger the ability to look through a window into their garage? I wouldn't want that, and I was sure Mr. Alexander didn't either. A minor detail like that wasn't going to stop me. I knew the outside appearance of the house looked just like mine. So, I was pretty sure the inside was very similar. If I was right, then the door to the garage was situated right inside their kitchen. The backyard was next on my list to check out, which was most likely a straight shot to the garage.

I gripped the bottom of the ski mask and pulled it down over my face.

Thank you, Alicia. Let's hope this works.

I ran around the house to the backyard. I needed to work quickly to avoid being seen. My feet skidded to an abrupt stop. My eyes were fixated on a horrific scene, fresh out of a horror movie, only it was still daytime.

There were two shovels lying on the ground with another standing up in a fresh pile of dirt. I stared at in intensely. The mound looked like someone had dug a hole and filled it. I swore it was a grave. The only item missing was a tombstone. My mind instantly wondered if Bethany Alexander lay buried under that mass of soil. I inched towards the mound timidly. The closer I got, the more I realized the hole had not been large enough for a body to be sprawled out like a corpse.

Did he chop her up? Was this his way of getting rid of his wife? Or was this simply an attempt to conceal the evidence?

I whipped out my cell and snapped a few pictures.

Colton needs to see this.

I documented every bit of the backyard with photos. I loaded them into a message to send my husband. That's when my eyes noticed the black tarp lying on the ground, adjacent to the concrete by the back-door.

Why wouldn't he wrap the body in the tarp before burying her?

I approached with my phone in hand, snapping more pictures of the evidence. I needed to send everything to Colton. I needed the police to rip apart the backyard in hopes of locating Bethany Alexander.

I examined the tarp, finding crimson streaks all over it. I was sure the markings belonged to Mr. Alexander's missing wife. I added the pictures to the message and began typing Colton's name. Then, my phone vibrated in my hand.

Seeing Alicia's name sent my heart into my throat. "What's wrong?"

"Your neighbor just pulled into the driveway."

I had to think fast. I was standing in plain sight. He would see someone standing in the backyard the moment Mr. Alexander entered the house. I was sure he would call the police, or worse, he could have a gun stashed away in case of an intruder.

"Is he entering through the front door or the garage?"

"Neither; he's coming around the side of the house," she advised.

What do I do?

I was two seconds away from being busted by my suspect, and I had yet to break into the garage to see if his wife's car was sitting inside it. I considered throwing something through the glass door. It would give me the access to the house, and I could have made a mad dash for the garage. The noise would have alerted Mr. Alexander and caused him to come after me a lot quicker and with more aggression. My other option was to hop the fence and pray no one else saw me.

But then, a third option entered my mind. I removed the ski mask and the sweatshirt, tying it around my waist.

"What are you doing back here?" Mr. Alexander appeared seconds later with a disturbed look on his face.

I was quick to come up with an excuse. My interaction with him yesterday gave me the idea. "I knew you were planning to do some gardening. I rang the doorbell and no one answered. So, I came back here thinking you might have started. I figured I could help."

"I never said I was doing any gardening," he snapped. Apparently, he wasn't thrilled with me showing up uninvited and unannounced.

"Then, what are you doing with all that stuff?" I pointed to the shovels and the mound of dirt. "And what's with that tarp?"

I was already busted for snooping around. My suspect knew I found the instruments used to cover up whatever crime he had committed. I figured it would be best to push the envelope a little further to see what he would accidentally confess. I doubted there would be another opportunity.

"What I'm doing in my backyard, is none of your business." He reached into his pocket.

Oh God, am I about to die?

He held up his cell phone and stabbed at the screen while intensely staring me down. "I'm calling the police."

Couldn't he have just brandished a gun or a knife at me in a threatening way? Why did he have to call the cops?

My first instinct was to run, but there was nowhere for me to go. I lived directly across the street from the man. All he would have to do is wait for the police to arrive and direct them to my house. So, I stood in front of Mr. Alexander while he told the dispatcher about a neighbor trespassing on his property.

It was a minor offense, but it was enough to make them arrest me once they showed up. I decided to force an intervention on my behalf. I slipped my cell out of my pocket and sent a quick text to Alicia letting her know what happened and for her to call my husband.

It took fifteen minutes for the car to arrive. I could hear the angry whisper of a man walking towards us in the backyard. Seeing Colton appear in the entrance caused me to have mixed feelings. I was happy it was him. It was unlikely he would arrest me for this. At the same time, I could see the rage in his eyes. He wanted to tear me a new one for refusing to stay away from our neighbor.

Colton stood off to the side with Mr. Alexander. They were having a heated discussion over me trespassing on his property. A couple of times they pointed at me. Finally, they parted ways. My suspect entered his house from the backdoor, leaving Colton staring at me.

"I need to explain," I began.

He held up his hand to silence me. "I don't want to hear it right now. Mr. Alexander and I reached an agreement. He is not pressing charges *this* time. *But* you are never to step foot on his property again, or else he will have you arrested for trespassing and harassment."

I was a bit relieved to know I wasn't going to jail. The bigger problem was how I was going to gather evidence without getting busted again.

Colton escorted me back across the street to our house. Alicia was hanging out on the front porch watching me do the walk of shame, only this was more of a perp-walk.

"Serena, you're okay."

"Yeah, she's lucky you called me," Colton growled. "I'm surprised you let her drag you into her paranoid delusions. You're usually the levelheaded one. I expected you to snap her back to reality."

"I tried, but she was going to do this with or without my help," Alicia defended. "If she was right, then someone had to be here to watch her back."

And I was extremely grateful for her. Alicia used the in case of emergency card and made sure to send for the cavalry before I was carted off by one of his fellow officers.

Colton's eyes darted from Alicia to me. He pointed a finger of warning in my direction. "*You* stay away from Mr. Alexander."

"Yeah, but you need to hear what-"

"We can talk about it when I get home. I have to get back to work, protecting people from nutcases like you." He started to walk back towards his patrol car. "You both better stay out of trouble."

I nodded in agreement. Then, Colton turned and walked back to his car. I watched him drive away before Alicia and I went inside the house.

"So, what do we do now?" she asked.

"I need to wait for Colton to get home tonight. Hopefully, he will listen to me after I show him what I found at Mr. Alexander's house."

"But didn't he see it?"

"He was too busy talking our neighbor out of pressing charges than to worry about common items lying on the ground. He wasn't even close enough to the tarp to see the crimson streaks." I stared out the window at the house across the street, wondering if I blew the only chance I had to stopping a killer.

12

My husband darted back to his cruiser, rushing back to work. I was sure he'd rather be anywhere than near me. He cast one more anger-filled glance in my direction before slamming on the gas, speeding away from me. A massive fight was brewing between us, one where he had all right to be pissed off at me. I had used my get out of jail free card because I had been convinced my neighbor killed his wife and covered up the murder. Before trespassing, I had no evidence. Now, I had something to show Colton.

"How about I pick up Izzy from school?" Alicia suggested as I stood on the porch. "She can stay at my house for a surprise playdate, while you and Colton work through what happened today."

I nodded in agreement. "That would be great; thank you."

Alicia took her ski mask and bag full of clothes meant for her and left my house. She wanted nothing to do with the fallout. Who could blame her? My marital spat was not something she, nor my daughter, needed to witness. Alicia's offer was exactly what I needed. A night of freedom where Colton could express his frustrations with me, and I could do my best to convince him to look into Mr. Alexander a little more.

I closed the front door. The emptiness inside the house left an intense feeling of anger, ready to burst through the walls the moment my husband came home. In the meantime, I would be left in solitude, a silence to fill my mind with more theories and reasons for my neighbor killing his wife, along with counters to anything Colton had to say.

Instead of dwelling on things I could not change, I decided to clean the house and make dinner. There was no romantic gesture or meant to be an apology. The stress of the upcoming conversation drained my mental and emotional state. Cooking, cleaning, and baking had become my outlets for relief, which usually made my family happy. Plus, good food and a dessert was my ally in diffusing the situation.

The sun began to set over my house, indicating the hours that had ticked away since my earlier incident. I heard the sound of a car pulling into the driveway.

Here he comes. Get ready, girl.

I braced myself for Colton to storm into the house, looking to rip into me for my impulsive actions. I stood my ground, ready for the onslaught of words, laced with his anger. I deserved everything he had to say. I had gone against his wishes, broke into my neighbor's yard, and was almost arrested, had it not been for Alicia calling my husband.

I waited for the sound of the door banging against the wall, as it had done so the last few nights. This time, I barely heard anything. Colton opened the door quietly and closed it. I peeked around the corner and saw him tiptoeing towards the stairs, as if he was trying to sneak into the house like a teenager. Colton stopped as his head turned towards me. His eyes were locked onto mine.

"Is everything all right?" I asked.

His face contorted into an angry expression the moment I opened my mouth. I could see words, laced with hurtful reprimands, were on the tip of his tongue. I braced myself for the verbal lashing. I shut my eyes, waiting for the bass in his voice to fill the house."

"I just want to go upstairs and relax." I opened my eyes to see Colton breathing heavy. He was holding back. "I had a *really* stressful day." There was no yelling, but there was contempt residing in his voice as Colton continued up the stairs.

Something's not right. Where is the lecture on me investigating a potential crime? Where was the scolding words, telling me how lucky I was that Mr. Alexander didn't press charges.

I didn't need Colton to reprimand me. My brain was doing a good enough job all on its own.

I sat down in the kitchen, giving Colton a few minutes to unwind. I had hoped he would come downstairs on his own. After a half hour, I was still at the table, with dinner set in front of me, and a plate resting in front of my husband's empty chair.

I got up and marched towards the steps. "Dinner is ready." There was no response. I didn't know if he was up there showering or had fallen asleep. I ascended the stairs and poked my head into the room. He was lying on the bed watching T.V. "I don't know if you heard me-"

"I know," he replied coldly. "Dinner is ready." His focus was on the screen, refusing to take one second to look in my direction. "I ate on the way home."

"Oh," I said feeling like his words had punched me in the gut. We always ate as a family, and today he chose to grab his own food. "You could have called or texted to let me know."

"And here I thought that form of communication was only used when you need me to send a deputy to check into your paranoia, or for me to bail you out when you do something stupid."

That was low.

I could accept his anger and even a lecture, but I refused to stand there and be disrespected. Yes, I had my husband use his power and influence to stop Mr. Alexander from pressing charges, but I still believed I was right in my theory.

"I'm sorry you had to get involved. I tried to do the right thing. I called you first the other night." Colton finally snapped his head towards me. "I could have run out of the house in search for the screaming woman without letting you know."

"You were watching Izzy," he roared. "That's the *only* reason you didn't do something stupid."

He was right. Our daughter was the only thing stopping me the other night. Had she stayed with a friend or if my mother had been at the house, I would have rushed out to find out what happened.

"You're going to jump on me for being paranoid, but I did the responsible thing. It's not my fault you refuse to believe me."

Colton jumped off the bed. I could see fury in his eyes as he stared me down. "I'm a cop, Serena. I have to follow procedures. The facts showed there was no sign of a break-in, injury, or death. No one reported any incidents in our area except you."

"No, there was just a suspicious neighbor who purchased supplies that someone looking to get rid of a dead body would use. That same person has a wife who has been missing for days."

"Mrs. Alexander has been away on business."

"So, her husband claims, but has anyone confirmed that information?" I waited for him to respond but continued before Colton could say another word. "Don't you think it's a coincidence Bethany Alexander had a *work meeting*, which took her out of town, the same time I heard a woman scream?"

His cheeks were enflamed with boiling frustration. "This is all in your head, Serena."

"Really; why did Mr. Alexander suddenly need to buy a large amount of cleaning supplies? Why did he need brand new shovels and a tarp that had blood stains on it?"

"Not like it is any of your business, but Mr. Alexander was prepping his home for Halloween."

"No one waits until the last minute to decorate for a holiday."

Colton cracked a smile. The tension in his face slowly eased. "Mr. Alexander loves Halloween, but his wife hates it. Bethany Alexander is not a big fan of decorating for any holiday, let alone one that celebrates candy and costumes."

"He told you that?"

"He did," Colton replied. He approached and grabbed my hands gently. "You need to listen to me. There is nothing suspicious happening at the Alexander house."

"But the tarp-"

"I saw it, but did you notice the bottle of fake blood sitting on the table near the grill?"

That was something I failed to see. I replayed the time in Mr. Alexander's backyard. My focus had been on the shovels, the tarp, and looking for a way to break into the house. I wasn't concerned with anything else.

"That could have been planted there to throw you off."

Colton dropped my hands. "Do you hear the words coming out of your mouth? You sound like a crazy, conspiracy theorist, who only cares about her own opinion rather than the truth."

"And you're quick to believe a possible murder suspect instead of the only witness, and your wife."

I attempted to storm out of the room, but Colton quickly snatched my wrist. "Serena, wait-"

I turned around, hoping he would come to his senses. "What?"

"I need you to promise me you won't go anywhere near Mr. Alexander or his house again."

Is he serious? Why would I agree to that, knowing he was my prime suspect?

"We're done here. I have a dinner to eat by *myself*."

"I made a deal with him. I promised you wouldn't go near him or his home again. In return he wouldn't press charges."

I ripped my arm free and stomped towards the bedroom door.

"If you do, then he will have you arrested for trespassing and harassment. There won't be anything I can do to keep you out of jail." His words held me in place as I crossed the threshold and into the hallway. "Think of Izzy. I don't want her knowing you were arrested because you were too busy chasing your paranoia."

I slammed the door shut behind me and sunk to the floor, covering my eyes with the palms of my hands. I could feel the tears pushing against my skin, slipping through the cracks, and racing down my cheeks.

There was no way I was leaving that sweet girl behind. But how do I turn my back on a woman who cried out for help?

13

Chapter 13

The tension in the house could have been cut with a knife. Colton remained upstairs, locked away in our bedroom, refusing to come out and speak to me. I contemplated his words, while sitting in the living room. I had nothing to say to my husband. His final words to me cut deeper than him dismissing my feelings or my theories. He used our daughter to drive his point home, and it worked. I wasn't about to go anywhere near Mr. Alexander or his house, but that didn't mean I was about to give up my investigation either. I just needed to be more creative.

Two hours later, I received a text from Alicia, checking to see if the coast was clear. I texted her to let my friend know I was coming to pick up Izzy from her house. I had no desire to rehash everything between Colton and I. Doing so over the phone or at the house had the potential for Izzy to eavesdrop on the conversation. She didn't need to hear any of it.

I sat in Alicia's driveway for a few minutes, collecting myself, before venturing inside. Izzy jumped into my arms as if she hadn't seen me in days.

"Did you have a good night?" I asked.

"Yes, mommy." Her smile was ear-to-ear. "Thank you for the play-date." Her appreciation had been directed at Alicia and me.

I thanked my friend as well and decided to leave the pending conversation for the next morning. A simple nod confirmed her understanding.

We were home ten-minutes later. Izzy rushed into the house to see her daddy. Immediately, she brushed her teeth and dressed herself before Colton came in for their nightly routine. I managed to sneak in one quick kiss goodnight before slinking off to bed. It was the first opportunity I had to get into the room without interacting with my husband. I was in no mood for any further arguments and sleep had been calling my name for over an hour.

The sound of my alarm woke me. The decision to sleep through it weighed heavily on my mind. The consequences were harsher this time as opposed to earlier in the week. I was co-anchoring for the rest of the week, which meant I had to look stunningly ready for the camera.

I slid out of bed at twelve-forty-five and jumped into the shower. The blow dryer was kept on medium, to keep the noise from waking my husband. I flat ironed my hair, parting it in the center, and allowing it to fall perfectly even on my shoulders. The make-up application was a bit more than my normal appearance.

Halloween was only a few days away, which gave me the idea to dress a little more festive, without using a costume. I pulled a few items from the closet, sliding my orange, pencil skirt over my legs and up to my hips. My fingers fumbled with the buttons on my black blouse and paired them with matching four-inch pumps. I glanced at the time and noticed it was early enough for me to take care of my morning needs. The coffee pot had a fresh pot brewed, thanking the lord for programable devices. I took a slice of pumpkin pie, Alicia brought over the other day, and devoured it immediately.

I painted on my on-camera ready face at the station. It was quiet, hardly anyone was there just yet. Those who walked around were field reporters, getting set to head out for their assignment.

I really wish I was covering a story, instead of anchoring.

"Well, don't you look fancy?" I looked up from my mirror and saw Alicia walking over to my desk. She pulled up a chair next to me with a smile on her face.

"It's the price I pay to be chosen as the substitute co-anchor." I held up the notes I found on my desk that morning when I walked in. I could only assume Ben placed them there before I arrived. "I just want to get this over with, today."

Alicia inched closer, bringing her voice down to a whisper. "So, we didn't get to talk last night. Is everything okay between you and Colton?"

I shifted my eyes towards Alicia before going back to the mirror. "It wasn't our best night." I inhaled deeply and launched into the story. "So, I have been given an ultimatum; stay away from Mr. Alexander and his home, or I get an express ticket to jail for harassment."

I could see Alicia shaking her head at my words. "Please, tell me you're not going back there this afternoon."

"No, I'm not in the mood to be arrested, today."

"When has the threat of prison deterred you from investigating?"

"Colton told me there would be nothing he could do to stop the arrest. Then, he added Izzy to the mix, forcing me to think of her watching me taken away from her."

Alicia wrapped her arm around my shoulder. The tears pooled in my eyes. I ripped a tissue from the top of my desk, blotting my face, hoping I didn't ruin my make-up before going on-air.

"That's a sobering way to think about it." Alicia tightened her embrace. "He must have been really mad, if he used her to see his way of thinking."

"He's not wrong." The admission almost broke my heart. "I was dumb for thinking I could do this on my own. I mean; what if he wasn't around to bail me out? What if Mr. Alexander decided to press charges and had me arrested? Izzy would have been stuck at school, and Colton would have had to explain to our daughter why mommy wasn't coming home."

Alicia expelled a deep breath. "So, does this mean you're dropping the whole investigation?"

That was the question I asked myself repeatedly since last night. I had no leads, no evidence, and no reports of an incident near our house. There was nothing supporting my accusations, but a part of me knew something happened and didn't want to let it go.

"I don't think I have much of a choice."

Alicia patted my arm in a consoling way, as if letting go of the investigation was the same as losing someone close to me. "You're doing the right thing."

Am I?

In my heart, I was choosing the option that was best for my family. But I couldn't help but listen to the other part of me, the one that knew there was a woman who had been in trouble. Maybe it was Bethany or possibly someone else who called out for help. I was the only one who heard her, and I was the only one willing to do something about it.

There has to be another way for me to do this.

My attempt to strategize was cut short as Ben strolled into view with a big smile on his face. "Good morning, Serena. Have you had a chance to read over your notes for this morning?"

"I was just about to do it, sir."

"Perfect. We should be ready to get your mic pack on and run a test in about ten minutes."

"Sounds good."

I gave a big thumbs up with a fake smile to show I was being a team player. Meanwhile, I want to stick a different finger in his face. I really wanted to be out in the field covering a story, any story would suffice. Instead, I was forced to sit at a desk on camera for the next few hours, trapped in my own thoughts with no one to talk to other than a camera and my co-anchor.

"I guess you have work to do," Alicia said as she stood up from my desk. "I'll catch up with you later."

The next half hour flew by. It was as if my mind and body were flying on autopilot. By the time I snapped out of it, I found myself sitting at the news desk. There were five minutes until showtime. I had to prepare myself for the next few hours of being on camera reporting the news.

The first segment leading to the break was filled with traffic, weather, and our top stories. There wasn't anything out of the ordinary. More shootings in Dekalb County; another robbery; and more political topics that I was sure no one wanted to hear about. We stopped taping, which gave me two minutes to chug down a bottle of water before the red light came on. I sat there staring into the lens as I read another story that shook me to my core.

"Police are still searching for a missing woman in Peachtree City." I stopped immediately and stared blankly into the camera. "Shareem Kinsley, a twenty-five-year-old woman, was last seen by her family Monday night, and believed to be meeting up with her friends at a local bar." The picture of the missing woman was displayed on the screen. I could see it on one of the monitors behind the camera crew. "Police are asking you to contact them if you have seen her."

The full weight of the story hit me the moment the camera shifted to my co-anchor. He continued reading from the teleprompter while I tried to grasp what I just told the viewers.

There was a woman who went missing the same night I heard someone scream.

I wasn't one to believe in coincidences. I was sure the two incidents were related. In fact, I was sure they were the same person.

I continued reporting the news for the next few hours, trying my best to push away the nagging thoughts, which begged me to dive right back into my investigative theories.

Seven o'clock couldn't come fast enough. I bolted from the chair the moment the red light on the camera turned off and we were free to roam around for the next half hour. I ran to my desk, kicked off my heels, and began to do a search on Shareem Kinsley.

I found out she lived on Turnbridge Circle. Her home was a few minutes away from Highway 74. There were many businesses and bars in that area she could have gone to.

A little voice inside my head, sounding like Colton, chimed in. *You don't know what was going on with her. She could have run away. She could have hitchhiked somewhere or met up with friends.*

The little voice made valid points. It was wrong to jump to conclusions, but that just meant I had to go into full reporter mode to get the answers.

I called Alicia while I still had time before the national show cut over to our local station for the top stories and weather.

"Hey, did you know about that missing woman?"

"Not really," she replied. "I heard it mentioned on the news when we got back to the station on Tuesday but that was it." She paused as if the light bulb clicked on in her head. "You don't think this has something to do with that scream you heard, do you?"

"I don't know, but I need to do some digging around."

"Serena, this is an actual investigation. You need to let the police handle it."

"I'm not going to do anything illegal."

"Uh huh," she replied. Obviously, Alicia didn't believe me. "The last time you said that; you tried breaking into your neighbor's house."

"I'm only going to do some research on the missing person and maybe visit her friends and family to find out what she was doing or was supposed to do that night."

"A camera crew already went out there, and the police have probably questioned them to death."

"Yeah, but none of them can get someone to talk like I can." I had a knack for convincing people to open up to me. It just didn't work all the time.

"Why do I get the feeling you're going to drag me into this too?"

"You're my photographer; of course you're coming with me. If I show up alone, then they'll think I'm some crazy person who is trying to pry into their lives."

"Serena, you are a crazy person trying to pry into their lives."

"True, but I have good intentions." I waited for Alicia to send another snarky comment my way but was met with dead air. "So, are you with me?"

I was met with silence. I almost thought call ended or we lost the connection. Finally, Alicia let out a sigh.

"Sure, I'll meet you at the station in a bit."

"Great, I'll see about getting clearance from Ben to work the story."

Chapter 14

Every moment between on-camera appearances was spent researching Shareem Kinsley. Her social media accounts were a wealth of knowledge, providing me insight into her background. I found out she graduated McIntosh High School in 2010 before venturing off to college. She obtained her degree from Kennesaw State, where she studied to be an elementary school teacher. After obtaining her license, she began teaching at Peachtree City Elementary, where she had been employed for the last three years.

My eyes flickered to the corner of my computer, noting the time. I had fifteen minutes before I was due at the news desk. I glanced up and noticed Ben walking towards his office. It was the perfect time to pitch my idea to run a special report on Shareem. I wanted to use it as my excuse to investigate her disappearance, but I also wanted to give her story enough exposure where someone could help the police locate her.

"I don't know about this, Serena." Ben was not a fan of special interest stories. He was more concerned about ratings and outscooping other networks. "We ran the story a few times since Tuesday. There hasn't been a single person who came forward with any information. My contacts at the police department haven't received any tips."

"That's *exactly* why we need to do this story." I shut the door to his office, not wanting the rest of the station to hear us. "We need to give Shareem and her family more airtime." I could see Ben was ready to dismiss my idea. "Hear me out before shutting this down."

He nodded. "You have two minutes."

"Most viewers are preoccupied with getting ready for work or school. They don't notice anything other than top stories, the weather, traffic, and sports. The stories we ran for Shareem have been two or three minutes long."

"We have an obligation to report news. We can't just focus on a girl who may have run away."

"She didn't run away." I was adamant in proving that theory wrong. Even if Shareem wasn't the woman connected to the scream, I was sure something had happened to her.

"What are you proposing, Serena?"

"Let me interview her friends and family. We can run the footage during the day and set up a lengthier airing at night. We put a spotlight on who Shareem is; where she went to school; her hobbies; her career as a beloved elementary school teacher; and where she hung out. Maybe someone ran into her recently and they haven't seen the two-minute reports where we mentioned she was missing. Maybe they were the last person to see her before Shareem went missing. Our in-depth story could reach a person who has vital information needed to find her."

"I get it; you want to help this girl."

Ben didn't understand, but I was determined to make him see my point. "No, we need to help her. Too many women of color go missing every day because they were mixed up with the wrong people or targeted for human trafficking. They get a quick mention on the news, if that, and coverage switches to something like politics. These girls aren't provided an opportunity to be saved. *We* have a chance to do something to help Shareem Kinsley and her family."

Ben sat with his mouth open. "Serena- I-I just don't have anyone we can spare for this story."

"I'll do it."

The smile on his face confirmed he wasn't going to buy into my proposal. "I appreciate you volunteering, but I need you for the morning show."

"I'll work on it after my shift is over. I'll take care of the anchoring duties in the morning, and I'll take Alicia with me to interview everyone on our own time."

"I'm not paying overtime."

"We're not asking for it. I just want to help find this woman."

Ben threw his hands in the air. There were no more reasons or excuses why I couldn't conduct the interview.

"Fine, do whatever you want, as long as it's done on *your* time."

"Thanks, Ben; you won't regret it."

There was a renewed spring in my step as I rushed back to my desk. Alicia was already waiting in my chair with a look of confusion on her face.

"You look a lot happier than this morning."

"I just spoke to Ben about our little project." I raised an eyebrow and smiled. "We have the green light to investigate Shareem Kinsley's disappearance. We just need to do this outside of our normal working hours."

"So, we're doing this for free?"

"Do you want to find Shareem or not?"

Alicia let out a deep sigh. "Just promise me we won't need to call your husband to bail us out."

"We will be very professional, especially since Ben is expecting us to put together a story for the nightly news."

Alicia got up and flattened out her pant legs. "Okay, I'll load up the van with my equipment. We can go as soon as you're done with your shift."

My final scheduled on-camera appearance signaled the end of my co-anchoring responsibility for the day. I finished up a few odds and ends over the next hour before I was given the green light to go after the real story.

My heels clicked aggressively as I ventured down to the loading bay, where Alicia had been waiting. She glanced up from the rear of her van as I approached.

"All set? Where should we begin?"

"I think it would be best to start with her family. This way, they can be made aware of our station doing a special interest piece on Shareem. Maybe they can help point us in the right direction for possible leads or advise who else we can speak to about her life. Her friends might be our best chance to find out what happened.

Alicia hesitated as she got into the driver's seat. "Didn't someone already go to her family's house and interview them? Won't they find it bizarre another reporter from the same network is coming to ask them a bunch of questions?"

"You're right; they could find it suspicious. Her family could question our motives and shut this whole project down right away, but I really doubt they will stop us. I would think Shareem's family would do everything possible to find her."

I would hate to think about something happening to anyone in my family, especially Alicia. I would move every mountain on earth to find them and their abductor.

"Fine, but don't expect me to hold back the *I told you so* once they tell us to go away."

Alicia and I got in the van and drove towards Peachtree City. It took us a half hour to arrive at Turnbridge Circle. I jumped out of the passenger seat and glanced back at Alicia.

"Come with me but leave your equipment."

"Why?"

"Do you really want to introduce ourselves by shoving a camera in their face as soon they open the door?" I needed to show the Kinsley family respect, especially during a difficult and stressful time. "Just follow me. I'll take the lead."

I rang the bell and introduced myself and Alicia to Ms. Kinsley, Shareem's mother.

"I already spoke to a slew of reporters earlier this week. Unless you have something to tell me, then I have nothing more to add."

Alicia was trying hard not to let her smirk show. I wasn't about to let a simple decline to comment stop me from helping the Kinsley family find their loved one.

"I understand, but we're not here to see what else you know about the other night. I requested to do a piece on your daughter to shine a light on who she is and why people should care about her."

I could feel Ms. Kinsley staring a hole thru me. I couldn't tell if she thought I was telling the truth or full of it. "Why? What do you get out of learning more about my baby?"

"To be honest, missing person stories don't get the attention they deserve. I want to help break that cycle by making sure our viewers know who Shareem Kinsley is and hope one of them can help us find her." I had to believe this woman was still alive.

Her expression softened. A single tear formed in the corner of her left eye. "Thank you," she sobbed. "Please, come in and have a seat in the living room."

I advised we would be a moment before heading back to the van. Alicia and I grabbed her equipment and brought it into the house, where we set it up near the couch. Ms. Kinsley showed up with a small box of cookies she set on the coffee table.

"Can I get you ladies anything to drink?"

"Water would be great, thank you."

Ms. Kinsley disappeared into the kitchen and returned with two bottles. She set them down next to the box of cookies before sitting down on the opposite side of the couch.

"Let me know when you are ready, Mrs. Kinsley."

She gave a nod of approval, which signaled for Alicia to step behind the camera and begin recording. I opened the conversation up to allow Ms. Kinsley to talk freely about her daughter, especially things people might not know about her.

"My baby loved volunteering. She was always working at a shelter, serving food to the hungry, or spending time being a mentor to younger kids."

"Has she always been so generous with her time?"

"Oh, yes, ever since she was a kid. We spent countless weekends at our church, helping with their events, organizing the food dropped off by the parishioners, and worked as an usher during weekend service."

"Did her desire to do good deeds continue during and after college?"

"Shareem worked at soup kitchens a few times a month. She was at one last weekend." Ms. Kinsley got up from the couch and walked off-camera and into another room. She returned moments later holding a day planner, where she opened to the recent entries. "That girl always had too much going on, and she loved every minute of it."

Ms. Kinsley handed me the book, allowing me time to skim through the pages. Each one had potentially useful information. I wanted to take it with me, but I knew this could be misconstrued as tampering with evidence.

"Would you mind if I make copies of the entries? I would love to show examples of her service to the community."

Ms. Kinsley took the day planner from my hands. "I will make you copies, right now." She darted into another room and remained there for several minutes.

I didn't mean for her to do it, now.

Alicia stopped recording and hurried to my side. She bent down in a whisper. "Do you really think there's something in there that might tell us what happened to Shareem?"

"It's possible, but I want to use it to set up an accurate timeline of events leading to her disappearance. It could also show us who she was with during those entries."

Ms. Kinsley returned with a stack of papers resting in the crook of her arm. She handed them to me as if they had been a baby handed off to another person.

"I hope these will help with your story."

I thanked her again before slipping the stack of papers into my bag. I decided to steer the conversation towards Shareem's career.

"As I understand, Shareem graduated from Kennesaw and has been teaching at Peachtree City Elementary School."

"Yes, she loved kids. Shareem always wanted to better her community, and believed the change needed began with the youth. It was why she volunteered as a mentor to kids of all ages, and why she wanted to teach elementary. She wanted to be there to show kids they could do anything if they worked hard enough."

We stayed on the topic for another couple minutes, touting her success as a teacher. Hearing about Shareem warmed my heart. She seemed like an amazing woman, who fought to make something of herself while giving back to her community.

I decided it was time to switch to a new topic, Shareem's relationship with her mother.

"Mothers and daughters typically share a lifelong bond. Many instances, there is a friendship formed from their love for each other. It seems you and Shareem fell into that same category; am I correct?"

"We were practically inseparable while she was growing up. When she went off to college, we spoke every day. She moved back here after college to take care of me when I had fallen ill a few years ago."

"I'm so sorry to hear. How are you feeling?"

"I'm doing much better now, thank you. I had a small tumor, which had been removed. It took me some time to get back on my feet, but Shareem made sure I didn't have to worry about any bills. She took care of me and all my expenses."

That statement worried me. Teachers didn't make nearly enough to cover major hospital bills, such as electric, cable, water, and mortgage. I wondered how she managed to handle everything.

"You said Shareem spoke to you every day. Do you know if she was seeing anyone romantically?"

I was hoping Ms. Kinsley could provide something I could use. Maybe Shareem was seeing someone who helped her with her mother's bills.

"No," she dismissively replied. It was as if the notion was absurd. "Shareem barely had time to see her friends, let alone a man."

That was not the answer I wanted to hear. The quick dismissal had me wonder if there was somebody she didn't approve of, which could lead to a possible suspect.

Maybe Shareem was seeing someone without her mom knowing. Kids aren't a hundred percent truthful with their parents, especially when it comes to dating. Is it possible Shareem has a secret or two waiting for us to uncover?

I decided to leave any questions pertaining to a romantic partner alone, for now. I wanted to re-focus my attention on the last time Ms. Kinsley saw her daughter.

"Do you know where Shareem was going the night she went missing?"

The happiness in Ms. Kinsley's face faded. She was forced to relive the night her daughter disappeared. I could see the tears forming in her eyes once again.

"She made plans with some of her friends to meet for dinner and drinks. I think they were supposed to go around seven."

"Do you know which of her friends was Shareem supposed to meet with and where they were going?"

I watched Ms. Kinsley write down a list of names, but she was unable to tell me which restaurant they were meeting at or what their plans were for after dinner.

This brought me to the most difficult question to ask. "Do you know of anyone who would want to hurt your daughter? Did she have any enemies, or was there someone in her life she may have had an altercation with recently?"

Ms. Kinsley's eyebrows rose in a suspicious manner. "You're beginning to sound a lot like the police."

Well, I watched enough cop dramas to know what to ask. Plus, my husband is the sheriff.

"I'm sorry, ma'am. I just want to make sure I cover everything in hopes of finding your daughter."

"My baby was one of the nicest, sweetest people you'd ever meet. There wasn't a single person who could say anything bad about her."

My latest line of questioning was wearing out our welcome. I had pushed Ms. Kinsley further than initially intended, and she had been accommodated us in every way. I doubted there was much more she could tell us.

I glanced at the list, seeing there were several names listed, all were considered potential witnesses or suspects for me to interview. They were my next stop in the investigation.

Alicia and I spent the next few hours tracking everyone down. Unfortunately, they told me the similar stories that Mrs. Kinsley said. They had great things to say about Shareem and advised no one had a negative thing to say about their friend. When asked about a potential boyfriend, most denied Shareem had a love interest. Only one of them had a hunch there was someone special in Shareem's life.

"Why do you think she had a secret boyfriend?" I asked.

"She ditched us a few times," her friend, Francine told us. "The others didn't think much of it, but I knew Shareem wouldn't bail unless there was a really good reason."

"Has this happened in the past or only recently?"

"There had been a few times, but Shareem only did so when something important came up. Lately, she told us she was too tired or had stuff to do for work."

"So, you knew something was wrong?"

"I believed her, at first. Shareem was usually very upfront with us. Honestly, I didn't even think she had the ability to lie."

"How did you know she was lying?"

"I stopped by her house. She claimed to have a headache, and I wanted to check on her like she had done for us so many times. When

I got there, her mom seemed shocked to see me. Ms. Kinsley said Shareem told her she was going out with her friends. No one from our group knew where she went."

"What did the rest of the group think?"

"They shrugged it off," Francine replied. "I kept my suspicion and saw followed her one night. She was at a bar, alone. I wanted to go in but I figured she was meeting someone there."

"Why didn't you blow up her lie?"

"Of all people, Shareem deserved to have a secret all to herself. She was there for everyone. It was about time she lived her life."

I thought back to the questions I asked Ms. Kinsley. I wanted to know more about the night Shareem went missing.

"One more question. Her mother said Shareem was supposed to meet with friends for dinner and drinks. Can you tell me which bar you were headed to the night she went missing?"

The question seemed to confuse Francine. "We didn't have any plans with Shareem on Monday. We never partied that early in the week."

"What about meeting up for dinner?"

She shook her head. "We were usually busy with work during the week. Thursdays were reserved for dinner. Fridays and Saturdays were spent bar hopping." Francine tilted her head. A thought must have popped into her head, because she stared off into space. "If Shareem did go out to a bar on Monday, then I might know where she went." Her pause had me on the edge, almost begging for the information. "I think she went to Tavern."

"What makes you think she would go there?"

"It was her favorite bar. That was her *go to* place whenever we tried to plan our bar nights."

"Thank you. I'll check it out."

We left Francine and began our journey back to the station. Alicia may have been the one behind the wheel, but silence seemed to be the one driving the van. No one uttered a single word until we returned to the loading bay.

"Do you want to tell me what you're thinking?" Alicia finally asked.

"Why would Shareem keep her dating someone a secret from her mother and her friends?"

"Maybe they were too involved her personal life, and she wanted to see where things went with this guy before telling them."

That was a plausible scenario. I was sure there were many people who didn't want to bring their partner around their friends and family until they knew the relationship was something serious. I had wanted to believe that theory but my brain was already working on another possibility. It had a tendency to lean to the extreme as if it decided to jump out of a plane on a whim.

"What if the guy didn't want her talking about it?"

"So, you think he forced her to keep it a secret?"

"Exactly," I replied.

Alicia didn't seem to dismiss the suggestion. She let me chase the hypothesis. "I guess it's possible, but why?"

I believed most men were open about who they dated, especially if the girl they were seeing was very attractive, great in bed, or they were considered wife material. People who protected their dating life had something to hide.

"What if he was married?" The suggestion was blurted out before I had a chance to put on my filter.

Alicia rubbed her forehead vigorously. "I don't think I like where this is going."

"Think about it. It would be the perfect reason for a guy to request Shareem keep their relationship quiet."

"We don't even know for sure she was seeing someone."

"No, but we can easily find out."

Alicia's head turned towards me. Her eyebrows scrunched together in a confused expression. "What do you mean?"

"I think you and I need to go check out that bar tonight."

15

Chapter 15

It was back to the same routine. Picked up Izzy from school; helped her with homework; made dinner; waited for husband to come home. Colton barely said two words since walking through the door. I was afraid to speak, believing anything I said would ignite an argument. The only conversation occurred when Colton questioned Izzy about her day at school. They spoke for several minutes before the kitchen filled once again with an uncomfortable silence.

"How was your day?"

No other voice responded. I thought it was repetitive for him to ask Izzy again. I looked up from my pork chop and noticed Colton was staring at me.

"It was fine." There was a bit of shock and hostility etched in my voice as I responded.

Colton ducked his head low and looked down at his plate. My message had been apparently received. There was no need for an explanation. He knew he was still in the doghouse for the way he spoke to me last night.

"I caught you on T.V. this morning." Colton has never mentioned anything about the news, especially seeing me covering a story. I had anchored the news several times over the last two years and never discussed it. "You did a great job at the news desk." Colton was definitely trying to sweet-talk his way through the wall I had put up. He must have believed charming me was the way to lower my defenses. "Is this a permanent thing, or is it a temporary assignment until someone comes back?"

He wasn't about to let the conversation end. I wasn't in the mood to be answering Colton's questions, but I was curious to see where he was going with them.

I placed my fork on my plate, trying my best to convey an annoyed expression. "I am just filling in this week. I'll go back to field reporting on Monday."

"Do you like anchoring?"

No, I'd rather be out where the action was, instead of sitting behind a desk talking about the news before kicking it over to another reporter.

"It's not bad," I replied sharply. "I just miss traveling around with Alicia in the van, reporting on a variety of stories."

Colton nodded his head while shoveling food into his mouth. Silence quickly made its return to our table until Izzy finished her dinner. She got up and placed her dish in the sink like a good girl.

"May I be excused?"

"Yes, baby girl," I replied.

She hurried off to the living room and turned on the T.V. Once she put on a movie, I knew she would be focused only on the screen and nothing else. I decided to take that opportunity to mention the missing person's case I was investigating.

"What do you know about Shareem Kinsley?"

Colton dropped the food off his fork and almost bit into the metal side of it. "You know I can't discuss an ongoing case."

I knew he was going to take it the wrong way but I needed his help. "I wasn't asking about *your* investigation. I wanted to know what you learned about her as a person. The station has me doing a special interest piece on Shareem Kinsley. We're hoping it will help find her."

Colton wiped his face with a napkin. "That's really nice, but I still can't discuss anything with you." He got up from the table and started to walk away. I could see the wheels turning in his head causing him to linger near the entrance to the living room. He returned to the kitchen moments later. "What have you learned about her so far?"

I smirked at his hypocritical question. "Oh, you refuse to tell me anything because it's an ongoing investigation, but it's perfectly fine for me to divulge everything I know?"

He didn't seem to find my comment amusing. He folded his arms over his chest, while glancing back to ensure our daughter wasn't listening.

"Serena, if you have any information that could help with this case, then you are obligated to tell the police immediately."

"You know I would tell you if I had something credible." I wanted to toy with him a little more. It was fun to watch him almost beg for information. "Right now, I only have suspicions."

I could see the look in his eyes. I had him on the hook and could easily reel him in.

"I'm all ears." Colton leaned across the table, as if he expected me to give up my information without protest.

No, you need to work for this one.

"Now, you're interested in my theories? You haven't had the time or desire to listen to my suspicions all week."

"That was different, Serena. You claimed to hear a random woman's scream. There was no evidence of anyone being hurt or injured. We didn't find a crime had been committed, and nothing had been reported. This girl is *actually* missing."

Everything he said was true, but that didn't excuse him from dismissing my concerns as nothing more than a figment of my imagination.

"Did you ever consider the two incidents could be related?"

"You're saying the scream you heard could have been our missing person?" I could see Colton was beginning to think back on our previous conversations. Maybe he was putting the pieces together quicker than I could. "Do you have any evidence to support she was in our area?"

"No," I growled, knowing he was about to throw away the notion. "I was just saying it was a possibility. She could have also run away to start her life over or taken a vacation and forgot to tell everyone she was leaving."

I was willing to come up with every asinine possibility just to piss my husband off. His cheeks were glowing red. Steam was about to billow from his ears.

"If this is all you have, then we're done here."

Fun time was over. While I enjoyed riling Colton up, I needed to work with him if I planned on getting him to open up to me about Shareem Kinsley's case.

I let out a sigh. "Fine, I spoke with her mom and friends earlier today. No one could tell me of any known enemies."

"That's typical. Everyone claims the missing person is a saint, unless they have something against a random person in their lives."

I let out a chuckle. "Yeah, but I actually believe that in Shareem's case. Everyone I spoke to told me how amazing she was and how much charity work she did."

Colton shrugged off the information as if it had no meaning. "What else did you find out?"

I bit my tongue. I really didn't want to share the one item I managed to pull from my interview with Shareem's friends. I doubted I could win Colton over without using it.

"One of her friends believes Shareem had a secret boyfriend."

He lifted his head instantly. "Wait, who told you that one?"

I guess I did know something the sheriff didn't. "It was one of her friends. I can't remember which one."

Colton stomped towards me. His body language presented an intimidation factor I wasn't used to seeing.

"Don't mess around, Serena. No one mentioned anything about a secret boyfriend." He stared off into space and seemed to think out loud. "That could be the key to finding her."

He was right. It was pertinent information which could have been used to find Shareem Kinsley. As much as I enjoyed holding it over Colton's head, I needed to come clean with everything I knew.

"Her name is Francine, and she wasn't sure Shareem was seeing someone, but she suspected it."

"What does she base it on?"

"Shareem never bailed on her friends, at least not without a reasonable explanation." I was sure it was nothing substantial, but I had hoped Colton would find value. "Francine told me Shareem had been flaking out on the group a few times over the last couple of weeks."

"That could have been for any number of reasons." There was my skeptical husband. He was already trying to poke holes in the information I provided.

"I agree, but her mother told me Shareem was supposed to meet up with her friends the night she went missing. Francine advised they never hung out on a Monday."

"It could have been another group of friends," he replied. "Maybe she was going to see co-workers."

"It's possible, but why would she lie to her mother? Why would she ditch her main group of friends just to hang out with co-workers? And if she did, then why not just tell them like she had when something else came up?"

"Those are some good questions. I'll be sure to ask them when I re-interview all of Shareem's friends."

"And you'll let me tag along when you question them?"

"No," he said sternly.

"Okay, but can I come with you and stay in the car?"

"No."

"Well, will you at least tell me what you find?"

"You know I can't divulge any information about an ongoing investigation. I could get in some serious trouble over it, especially since you are a reporter."

Good to know he can use me for information, but he won't reciprocate and tell me anything in return.

I got up from the table and cleared the dishes. "I get it." My words were short and meant to sound snippy.

"Thank you for telling me what you found out."

"Uh huh," I replied.

"I mean it." Colton came up behind me and put his hands on my waist. "I promise; when this is over, I'll be sure to give you the exclusive interview with our police department."

I don't need your exclusive. I plan on getting my own.

"That's nice." I pushed his hands away and finished loading the dishwasher. "Oh, I forgot to tell you; Alicia and I are going out tonight."

He stopped mid-step and stared at me. "Where are you ladies going?"

"Out," I snapped. I shoved the dishwasher door closed and marched towards the stairs.

He tried to follow me like a concerned puppy, trailing after their owner. I headed up to the bedroom and picked out a knockout outfit, fitting for a girl's night out, and one that would have Colton kicking himself in the rear for how he treated me.

"What do you mean, out? Where are you going?"

I placed my clothes on the bed and glanced over at him as he stood in the doorway. "Honey, I can't divulge any information about an ongoing investigation." I smiled and entered the bathroom, closing it behind me.

16

Chapter 16

I emerged from the shower into an empty bedroom. I considered toying with Colton some more when I opened the door, but he must have gone downstairs to spend time with Izzy. That was probably for the best. Questioning me about going out would only lead to further arguments. The answers would upset him, and I didn't want Colton to talk me out of what I had planned. I was sure my husband would do everything possible to stop me if he knew my true intentions. There was a good chance of that happening when he saw the outfit I picked out.

I decided to get dolled up, using cherry-colored lipstick, bronzer, and fake eyelashes. I dressed in skinny, blue jeans, which clung to my legs and hugged my curvy waist. My satin, one-shoulder, black blouse, and candy-apple red pumps completed the look. Every step I took down the flight of stairs felt like the typical romantic comedy movie from the nineties, where the woman made a grand entrance to wow her crush. Colton jumped up from the couch the moment I hit the landing and walked towards the living room. His jaw dropped instantly, making every ounce of pain from my heels worth it.

Colton couldn't take his eyes off me. "You're not going out dressed like that." The growl in his voice sent a shiver down my spine.

I could picture my husband turning into a caveman, throwing me over his shoulder and carrying me back up the stairs, just to prevent me from going out. I could tell he wanted to put his foot down with an ultimatum of change or stay home. Colton may have been my husband, but he didn't own me, and I wasn't about to let him control anything about my night out.

"What's wrong with how I look?" I stepped to the side and glanced over at my daughter for her approval. "How do I look, Izzy?"

"You look hot, mommy."

"That's the problem," Colton snapped. "You look like you're going out to pick up a guy."

Guy or girl; it doesn't matter as long as they have information about Shareem.

"Alicia and I are just going out for a couple of drinks. We'll be home before you know it."

"Fine, give me ten minutes to get ready, and I'll go with you."

That was not part of the plan. Colton was supposed to stay home with our daughter. If he came out to the bar, he would ruin everything. Colton would go into cop mode, and he would prevent us from questioning anyone at the bar. Everyone knew he was the sheriff. No one would talk with him around.

"If you go, then who will watch Izzy?"

"We can call your mother."

I was quick on my feet. "She is out with her friends at a movie." There was a chance he would call me on my bluff, which meant I needed to sell it that much more. I pulled my cell from my clutch. "Do you want me to call her right now and tell her to ditch her friends because my husband isn't mature enough to let his wife go out for a couple of drinks?"

Colton and my mom had a love-hate relationship. Most of the time they were on good terms, but there were instances where my mother heard or saw something she didn't like and used it against him during an argument. I knew this was something he didn't want her knowing about.

He sat back down on the couch, sulking with his arms crossed over his chest. "Fine, go; have fun." His eyes flickered with anger with every step I took.

I walked out of the house and met Alicia at her car. "Everything all right?" she asked.

I glanced back at the house and saw Colton standing at the window, peering through the blinds. "Sure, if you count my husband overreacting to my outfit." I let out a grunt. "Me- husband- you- wife- too hot- guys hit on you."

Alicia laughed as we got in her car and drove off. "So, what's the plan for tonight?"

"I want to see who is there on a busy night. Someone might know Shareem. We can check with the bartenders too."

"Wouldn't it make sense to go when there are less people or go on the same night where she had gone missing?"

It was a valid question, but there were too many days between now and Monday. We couldn't wait that long to ask questions, which could have led us to finding her.

"Her friends said this was her *go to* place. This may be our best shot at finding information about what happened the night she went missing. At the very least, we could learn more about Shareem from unbiased people who weren't necessarily friends or family."

Tavern wasn't far from the house. It was a quick twelve-minute drive for us. Had I passed that nugget of information to my husband, he would have ensured deputies patrolled the bar all night. He probably would have instructed one of them to wait at the house with Izzy while he attempted to drag me home.

Stop worrying about Colton.

I shook him from my mind as Alicia and I approached the door. The music from the live band met our ears before entering the building. Large crowds of people had gathered inside.

A lot of people here tonight. That means a lot of possible witnesses and suspects for me to comb through.

"Should we split up?" I asked.

Alicia's eyes bulged at my suggestion, telling me that option terrified her. It wasn't an ideal choice for me either, but I figured it would be the best way to cover more ground.

"Do we have to?" I could hear the whining in her voice over the band rocking out to a song I heard in passing on the radio.

"No, just stick close to me."

We pushed our way over to the bar, grabbing a couple of beers before deciding to patrol the area. I searched for the best spot to *people-watch*. There was a great spot in the back, giving us access to see most of the people in the bar. The small perch also made it seem like we were checking out the band.

I felt Alicia's elbow nudge my side a few minutes later. "What do you think?"

"They're pretty good." I knew what she meant, but it was more fun to mess with her "We should come down here more often."

The back of her hand smacked my arm. "That's not what I meant. Have you seen anything that looks suspicious?"

"Oh," I replied in a tone to make it seem as if I had forgotten we were on a stakeout. I loved teasing Alicia. It was always so easy to mess with her. "I'm just kidding." I scanned the crowd, trying to find anyone who stood out. "There are a lot of people here. I don't know how quickly we would find-" My eyes locked on a man sitting alone at a table near the bar. I tapped Alicia on the shoulder and pointed out my number one suspect. "Mr. Alexander is here."

I am not one to believe in coincidences. I stood by the phrase *everything happens for a reason.* I stood in the bar where Shareem Kinsley had frequented often. And there, fifty feet away from us, sat the man who claimed his wife had unexpectedly left town on a business trip. I needed to confirm if both, Mr. Alexander and Shareem, had been seen at Tavern Monday night.

I marched over to the bar just as the band ended their set. I retrieved my phone and did a search on Shareem's name.

"Excuse me," I called over to the bartender. "I was wondering if you recognize this woman."

He nodded immediately. "She comes in here at least once a week."

"Were you working Monday night?"

"Yeah, I'm always on during the fall and winter schedule. It's one of the best shifts to work. There are just enough people to make good money, but I still have time to watch the games."

I assumed he meant football, but there was also the potential for baseball, hockey or basketball games on T.V. too. Mondays in October were mostly reserved for prime time on the gridiron.

"Do you know if she was here last Monday?"

"Shareem is here every week. She usually sits at the bar to watch the game while taking full advantage of our beer and wing specials." His eyes locked onto another patron who had signaled him. "Give me one minute; I'll be right back." The bartender darted to the man holding up a twenty-dollar bill. He poured two shots and placed two beers on the counter before taking the money from his customer. He returned a couple minutes later. "Can I get you anything?"

As much information as you are willing to part with before getting pissed off.

"Do you remember anything strange happening that night? Was there anyone hitting on Shareem? Did she have an argument with anyone?"

"No way," he replied instantly. "She was the sweetest girl. She came by every week, ordered the same thing, and tipped really well. Everyone here loved her, especially the guys."

That raised an eyebrow. "Did any of them hit on her?"

"She was a beautiful woman. I think there was at least one guy every week who asked her out or bought her a round."

I wasn't surprised to hear that bit of information confirmed. Shareem seemed like a very friendly woman who happened to be a knockout. Most men would find her attractive enough to shoot their shot.

"How many men were here Monday night?"

"Lady, I don't count the number of customers. I only care about how much they leave me for tips." He paused and stared at me. Curiosity burned in his eyes. "Why are you asking so many questions about Shareem? Are you a cop? Is she in some kind of trouble?"

Based on his questions, I doubted he was aware of Shareem's disappearance. I had the unfortunate task to break the bad news to him.

"I'm a reporter trying to help Shareem's friends and family figure out what happened to her."

"She's missing?" The shocked look on the bartender's face confirmed my assumption.

"Yes, and no one knew she came down here, and she hasn't been seen since Monday night."

"She was fine when she left the other night." His tone in his voice cried out defensively. I didn't believe him to be a suspect, but I had hoped he could provide me with some more useful information.

"What time did she leave here?'

"It was close to eleven-thirty."

That was an odd time for a teacher to be out on a school night. "Did she stay here that late every Monday?"

"It depended on the game. If it was a team she liked, then she stayed for the whole time and hung around long enough to sober up. If it wasn't someone she liked or her team did horrible, then she cut out by halftime."

I glanced around the bar. There were a few people I recognized from my neighborhood. My eyes locked onto Mr. Alexander again. "Have you seen anyone from that night here today?"

I could see he was getting annoyed by my questioning, but he tolerated me. My guess, he felt guilty to be one of the last few people who saw Shareem Kinsley before she went missing.

"There might be…I don't know. There are a lot of people here and some of them are regulars just like she was."

"One last question; can I get two more beers?"

He smiled and went back to his station to get us our drinks. I slipped him a twenty and told him to keep the rest. It was my way of thanking the guy for dealing with me. Plus, I had a feeling we would need his help again in the future.

Alicia and I turned to leave but stopped short when a man stood in my way. I almost bumped into him. The angry eyes of Mr. Alexander stared a hole into my soul.

"What are you doing here?" he growled.

"I'm just having fun with my friend. Is that a crime?"

"It is if you're here stalking me."

"I didn't know showing up a bar near my home was considered stalking." Alicia was trying to pull me away from my neighbor. She knew I was asking for trouble, but I was not about to back down from this man's intimidation. "I believe this is a public space and I am free to come and go as I please."

"You're only free because your husband, the sheriff, bailed you out before I could have you arrested."

He wouldn't have had to if you didn't murder your wife.

I kept those thoughts to myself and refused to move from my spot. I was already thinking of the next thing to say to get under Mr. Alexander's skin, but another voice interrupted us.

"Is there a problem here?" The bartender had slipped out from his post and wedged himself between us.

"No, no problem at all," Mr. Alexander replied. "It's just a friendly discussion between neighbors."

"Well, it doesn't look too friendly to me. So, I suggest you keep moving and leave the lady alone before security removes you from the building."

"Ha, another man rushing to your rescue. I'm sure you husband would love to hear that."

I wanted to slap the jerk for threatening to tell Colton some made up story. I knew that's what Mr. Alexander wanted me to do. There was no way I was about to give him that satisfaction, especially when he had plenty of witnesses to back up his story when he called the cops to have me arrested.

"At least my husband is there for me. When was the last time your wife did that for you?"

With that remark, I decided to walk away with Alicia. We scurried off into the crown, leaving Mr. Alexander behind.

Alicia gripped my hand tightly as we moved through the sea of people. "Why did you do that?"

"He provoked me first. I'm not backing down from someone who needs to feel strong and powerful by picking on a woman."

"Yeah, but I don't think that's a good idea if your theory is right. It's not like he's some stranger. He literally lives across the street from you."

I admit; it wasn't the smartest move, but it was enough to push my suspect a little closer to the edge. I just hoped it was the right amount to make him slip up.

17

Drinking in your thirties is not as much fun as partying in your twenties. The after effects were far worse than I remembered. The searing pain, threatening to burst the veins in my head, told me I had a severe hangover. My body felt like an eighteen-wheeler ran me over, and then dragged me for about fifty miles. Moving an inch on the bed seemed impossible.

That's it; I'm not getting up today. I'm just going to sleep until all this goes away.

Unfortunately, there were no days off from mommy-duty. I knew it was the weekend, and my daughter would be waking at any minute.

I crawled to the edge of the bed. My hand stretched out to grab my phone, knocking it to the floor in the process. It took two more minutes of pulling and dragging my old, thirty-eight-year-old body over the edge of the bed. I could feel my fingertips touching the screen, illuminating the device, displaying the time.

It's eleven-thirty. I slept the whole morning. Izzy must be starving.

Colton was not a good cook, not unless you counted his skills on the grill. He was a master with any cut of meat, no matter if he used charcoal, propane, or wood chips to cook the medley of food. I was sure he could fix breakfast on it as well, but he had never done it before. Plus, I didn't smell the distinct odor of flames engulfing whatever meat he threw on those greasy grates.

I slid my feet over the side of the bed and slipped down until I was able to stand. I stumbled twenty feet to the bedroom door and out into the hallway.

I listened for any sound coming from Izzy's room. I was met with silence, not even the faint noise from her T.V. My hand pressed on the wall for support as I walked down the hall. I made it just far enough to peer inside, finding her bed perfectly made and the room empty.

She must be downstairs.

It took me another ten minutes to travel down to the first floor. Each step felt like a huge accomplishment.

How do people do this on a weekly basis?

By the time I reached the landing, I noticed a blonde woman with hair hanging above her shoulders sitting next to Izzy. They were both on the couch watching a movie.

"Mom, what are you doing here?"

"Colton called and asked me to come over." I found that to be odd, since my husband didn't like to ask my mother for any favors. "He had witnesses to question about some case he's working on." She cracked a quick smile. "I was about to see what he was willing to offer in exchange, but then he told me you weren't feeling well." Her eyes scanned my physical appearance. "By the look of you, he downplayed it quite a bit. What's wrong?"

I took a deep breath and silently thanked my husband for being a good man. He made sure Izzy and I were both taken care of before running off to save the world.

"Thanks for coming over." I tried to enter the living room, but my feet seemed to remain rooted to the spot, causing me to stumble and fall. Izzy and my mother jumped up from the couch and ran to my side, helping me back to a standing position. "I'm okay," I told them. "I just got a little dizzy."

My mother tried to lead me to the stairs. "Maybe you should go rest."

"I should be fine after I eat and drink something."

My mother gave me a knowing look, as if she could see through my lies. I spent many mornings attempting to hide hangovers from her. I was sure she knew then, and I was sure she recognized it again. I was waiting for her to confront me and ask if I spent the night partying. We both looked at the concerned look on Izzy's face and decided to drop it.

"Why don't you go upstairs and take a hot shower? I'll fix you something and bring it up in a bit."

It felt like old times. My mom never ratted me out to my dad about my drunken escapades, and she didn't ground me either. She spent the time fussing over me until I felt better. I couldn't help but smile. For once, someone was taking care of me.

I grabbed a sports drink from the fridge before making my way up the stairs. The bottle was empty by the time I reached the second-floor landing. I drank the whole thing in less than a minute. The aches and pains were still there, but I was starting to feel slightly better.

I entered my room and stared at the bed. It was begging for me to dive face first into the pile of pillows. I could have curled up and fallen asleep within minutes. My orders were clear. I was supposed to wash up before my mother came up with food.

The hot shower seemed to wake me up even more. It felt refreshing. The steam cleared my mind, giving me the chance to think about last night. I remembered the conversation with Pete, the bartender, and the argument with Mr. Alexander.

What was he doing at the bar last night?

The thoughts consumed me while water rained down on my head. I needed to work through them with someone else to put them in perspective. That same person had to be someone who didn't think I was overreacting. Alicia was the only person who seemed to be on my side.

I turned off the shower and wrapped myself in a towel. My hand reached for the handle when I heard something inside my bedroom. I quietly opened the door, finding a man crouched down on the opposite side of the room. The safe door was wide open. It didn't look like they were taking anything out. Instead, they were putting a piece of paper inside.

I watched the man close the safe and turn around. "Geez, Colton; you scared me." I had to play dumb, as if I hadn't known the man in the room was my husband.

"How long were you standing there?" His defensiveness told me he had put something important in there he didn't want me to see.

"Not long," I replied. "I just got out of the shower." It was something he should have known. I always heard him turning off the faucet when it was his turn. Either he was playing dumb too, or he walked into the room just after I turned off the water. "What were you doing?"

"I-uh was locking up my gun."

He was a horrible liar. I could always tell when he tried to stretch the truth, even a little bit.

"Why did you have your gun out?"

"I was working. I always take it with me when I go out in the field or to the station."

"It's Saturday. You hardly ever work weekends."

"I was interviewing witnesses for a case I'm working on. I took my gun for protection."

Colton's body language confirmed he was telling the truth about interviewing people. Maybe he had taken the weapon with him, but he was fidgeting while casting glances back at the safe. He was nervous and defensive, as if there was something in that safe he was trying to hide or protect from me. I just needed him to leave so I could snoop around.

"Okay, great." We stood there in an awkward silence for two minutes until I decided to speak up again. "Do you mind if I get changed?"

"Sure, it's not like I haven't seen you naked before." His smirk told me he wasn't about to leave me alone with whatever was in that safe. Now, I was expected to give him a little show before Colton rushed me out of my own bedroom. "Yes, but our daughter is awake, my mother is here, and she is bringing me up food to eat in a few minutes because I'm not feeling well."

"Cut the act," he told me. "We both know you're not sick, Serena. This is just a hangover from your night out." He sat down on the edge of the bed staring at me. "So, where did you two go last night?"

"We went to a local bar." I placed my hands on my hips. "Is that a crime, sheriff?" I wasn't about to tell him Alicia and I went to the one bar Shareem frequented and was most likely the last place she had been seen.

"No," he scoffed. "I just hope you weren't out doing something stupid, like following our neighbor, whom I told you to stay away from."

I should have known Mr. Alexander was going to rat me out to Colton, especially once Pete ran interference and defended me. The tattletale put me in boiling, hot water with Colton. My only option was to come clean with the real reason I went to Tavern. It would be better for my marriage if Colton knew I was there investigating Shareem's disappearance rather than go against our agreement.

"I had no idea Mr. Alexander was going to be there last night."

"Out where?" Colton was pushing for me to admit everything and was using our neighbor to force a confession.

"Alicia and I went to Tavern. We were just trying to get some more information about Shareem."

Colton jumped off the bed. "*And-* what did you find out?"

I wasn't about to give up any more information to him. He wasn't willing to share with me, so I wasn't going to give up the goods.

"Nothing really," I replied. "She was there on occasion."

"Shareem was there more than just on occasion," he replied. "It was the place she went more than any other bar. It was her *go-to* place, especially to watch football."

I tried to scrunch up my face as if this information was new to me. "How do you she was there that much?"

"While you were sleeping off your night of partying and snooping, I was out speaking with Shareem's friends. I had each of them put together a list of bars and clubs they had gone to with Shareem in the last month. I also asked them to write down every place they knew Shareem frequented, even without her group of friends. They all mentioned Tavern and said Shareem Kinsley went there most Mondays to watch football. She also dragged her friends there on weekends."

"What other bars were on the list?"

Colton began laughing. "Sorry, I'm not letting you anywhere near that list. It is part of our investigation into Shareem's disappearance."

"Let me see it; maybe I can help."

"When you graduate the academy and have your own badge, then you can help me." We both knew that was not going to happen. I loved my job too much. "Until then, you are to stop snooping around, and let me handle the case."

"Yes, sir," I said with a salute. "Now, do you mind if I get dressed alone? I'd like to get ready without being ogled or interrogated."

"Sure," Colton replied as he made his way to the door to exit the room. He cast a suspicious glance at me before leaving.

I waited a few moments, listening for him to go downstairs. I heard him and Izzy speaking to each other, which meant I was free to poke my nose where it didn't belong. I punched in the code for the safe and saw there was a piece of paper sitting on top of his gun.

I carefully retrieved the paper and unfolded it. There were several notes listed. All of the bullet points indicated a different bar Shareem hung out at in the last month. There was one in particular which caught my eye. It was a place I needed to check out without Colton finding out.

18

Chapter 18

My cell phone sat on the nightstand, begging to be part of my devious plan to steal Colton's information. He was sure to be back any moment to check on me. There was no way my husband, knowing I was in the same room as his evidence, would let me have more than a couple minutes alone. I knew he would check it, immediately, making sure it hadn't been touched. Colton was so keen on detail; he would inspect the list to ensure it was in the exact same spot. It couldn't be off by even a centimeter.

My cell phone quickly became my accomplice. It took the photo, showing how the list was placed in the safe, just in case it was moved while I tried to review it. I used the device to take a few more snapshots of the information. Each move I made was quick, precise, and done with my brain trying to think of tricks Colton would use to prove I had looked at his evidence.

I shut the safe and began getting dressed, just in case my husband returned. When he didn't show right away, I decided to call Alicia.

"Hey, how are you feeling?"

Alicia let out a groan. "I feel like I got hit by a bus."

Trust me; the feeling is mutual.

Fatigue still raged through my body, demanding I collapse onto the partially made bed. Colton and my mother were both here to help take care of Izzy. It would have been easy for me to give in to the temptation of sleep, but Colton's list gave me the strength to push through the hangover and continue the investigation.

"Do you want to meet for coffee?"

"Uh-" Alicia dragged out the word as if she was lost in thought. "Yeah, I guess. Are you on your way over with Izzy?"

"Colton called my mother this morning to watch her while he went out for a bit. He just got home a few minutes ago." I paused, thinking it would be best for me to meet Alicia at her house for coffee, but homemade brew didn't sound as appealing as it being made by a barista. We also ran the risk of Alicia's husband overhearing us talk about the investigation. He would text Colton the moment he heard us mention Shareem Kinsley.

"There's a coffee place down the road from Tavern on 74."

"Fine," Alicia growled. I could hear her hand slap the bed, making me think she was still under the covers trying to hide from her day. "I can be there in a half hour. But if you get there first, then grab us a table."

Alicia didn't live far from our destination. A half hour was more than enough time for her to drag herself from the bed, wash up, throw on some clothes, and meet me at the coffee shop.

I, on the other hand, didn't have nearly enough time. I was sure Colton would be walking through our bedroom door any moment. I raced to get dressed before his arrival. I threw on a royal blue t-shirt, a pair of skinny jeans with a matching denim jacket, and a pair of ankle boots. It was one of my favorite fall outfits. I slowed down as I exited the bedroom and walked casually down the stairs.

Colton was playing with Izzy in the living room. He stared at me with curiosity burning in his eyes. "Where are you going?" His tone matched his facial expression.

"I'm going out for coffee." I tried to act as if it was something I already had planned prior to uncovering the list. "I'll be back in a little while."

Colton jumped to his feet. "We have plenty of coffee in the cabinet. You can make yourself a cup, or a whole pot, of it while you sit in the comfort of your own home."

His eyes were probing me for information. Every word I spoke, and every move I made, told him what I was really up to.

"I'm in the mood for something different, like an espresso. We don't have anything to make that here."

My husband was good at painting a suspect into a corner, but I happened to be one notch better than him. I managed to escape his trap with one statement. Colton was unable to counter my argument. He simply didn't know enough about coffee to outwit me in a battle concerning earth's greatest gift.

I watched him sit down next to Izzy. "Fine, can you pick me up something while you're out?" He raised an eyebrow, as if to say *check*. "I mean; you won't be long, right? You're hitting the drive-thru and coming right back?"

"Sure, I won't be long." It was a bold-faced lie, but I needed him to back off so I could meet up with Alicia. "Text me your order."

Internally, I was screaming at Colton. He was doing his best to limit my time, blocking me from my investigation. He would expect me back at the house sooner than I anticipated. He probably thought he had outsmarted me, but I had a few tricks up my sleeve.

I gave Colton and Izzy a kiss before leaving the house. My pace was slow and casual as I walked out the door to my car. I took my time backing out of the driveway, continuing the illusion that nothing was wrong. Once I was out of our community, I pressed my foot on the gas and rushed towards the coffee shop. I prayed Alicia was there when I arrived.

Her blue Honda sat in the parking lot as I located an empty spot. I nearly sprinted from my car, drawing attention from the other customers the moment I opened the door.

"What's wrong?" Alicia asked.

"Colton," I growled. "Come on; let's get our drinks and I'll tell you everything." I dragged Alicia onto the line as we waited to place our order.

I grabbed the Espresso Con Pana. Alicia asked for a Caramel Frappuccino. We both grabbed a spinach, feta, and egg white wrap and a chocolate chip cookie. Our investigation was getting more intense with each passing day, and I wasn't about to discuss a case on an empty stomach.

Alicia pulled me towards an empty table the moment we picked up our order. "So, what was so important you had to drag me out of bed to a coffee shop to discuss?"

I glanced around to ensure no one was listening. "Colton talked to Shareem Kinsley's friends this morning. He managed to get a list of all the bars they went to in the last month."

"That's a good thing, right?"

"Tavern was on that list."

"You shouldn't be surprised by that," she told me. "We already knew Shareem was there every Monday."

"Yeah, but did you know she also went to Crowe's Nest?"

Alicia held her Frappuccino to her lips, refusing to let any of the coffee enter her mouth. Her eyes stared at me, frozen in shock.

"Please, tell me you're joking."

I quickly whipped out my cell phone and brought up the picture I took of the list. I pointed out Crowe's Nest and the date Shareem's friends indicated they had last visited that bar.

I pointed to the screen again, emphasizing my thoughts. "She was there the same night Drinna Adams died in the parking lot. And Shareem just *happened* to go missing a few days later."

"It's probably a coincidence," Alicia suggested.

I tilted my head. *There is no such thing as a coincidence*

There were too many incidents linking everything together in such a short time span. I was sure they were all related.

"What if Shareem Kinsley saw something at Crowe's Nest that night? Maybe the killer saw her and decided to shut her up before she could place them at the scene of the crime."

Alicia broke off a piece of her cookie and pointed it at me. "You're really reaching on this one." She took a bite of the end while the silence fell between us. "Besides, Drinna Adams was found by one of her co-workers."

"Okay, maybe she didn't see the murder. Is it possible Shareem Kinsley witnessed someone stalking Drinna? Could she have overheard a conversation which could lead to a possible suspect?"

"Yes, it's possible, but I seriously doubt that's what happened."

"And what if I'm right?"

Alicia finished the piece of her cookie and stared at me with a serious look on her face. "Then, I think we really need to find out what happened to Shareem Kinsley, and by we, I mean you telling your husband what you know."

I hated the thought of giving Colton any more information about the case or my theories. He always seemed to laugh at them or shrug them off.

"Why should I tell him anything? He hasn't shared with me, and he won't work with us on this investigation."

Alicia patted the top of my hand gently. "That's because he's the sheriff and you're a reporter. He wants to keep you safe, and frankly, so do I."

I knew she was right, but there was no way I could go back to the house with my tail tucked between my legs and give up everything I uncovered.

"I can't tell him."

"Serena, you have to."

"You don't understand. I broke into his gun safe to get this information. Colton is going to flip out when he finds out I was snooping around his stuff."

"He's going to be more pissed if he finds out some other way." Alicia took a sip of her coffee and set it down quickly. "You need to swallow your pride and come clean about it. A woman's life is in jeopardy, and the three of us are the only ones who can help her before it's too late."

Alicia made a lot of sense, which helped me put things in perspective. Shareem's safety was our top priority. I had no other choice but to tell Colton the truth. He needed to know the connection with the bars, and what I suspected happened Monday night. I was sure he would yell and order me to stay away from his case. It wouldn't have been the first time, and I was sure it wasn't going to be the last time.

"Fine, I'll tell him when I get back to the house." I looked at my cell and noticed the time. Colton expected me back twenty minutes earlier, which meant I needed to race to the house. "Let me grab his coffee and rush home"

I stood up and walked back to the counter. There was an eerie feeling as if someone was watching me. I glanced over my shoulder a few times while standing on line to order, and again while I waited for Colton's coffee. My eyes searched the building for any sign of someone staring at me. Maybe Mr. Alexander was hiding behind the wall or a potted plant. I didn't see him. There were some familiar faces in the building but no one I recognized.

I grabbed Colton's regular coffee with milk and three sugars from the counter and rushed out of the building. I kept looking back to see if anyone came out after I left. My paranoia locked me inside my car with my eyes fixated on the rear-view mirror, waiting to catch someone searching the parking lot. It took several minutes for my anxiety to settle down. Once I felt safe, I turned the key in the ignition and drove home.

Colton sat in the backyard, on the deck, watching our daughter. Izzy sat in her swings, kicking her feet, as she glided through the air.

"I thought you were grabbing coffee from the drive-thru." My husband's tone was laced with annoyance.

I was willing to go all-in on my lie just to spite him. I could tell him in a half hour, bringing it up nonchalantly in conversation.

"The line was too long, so I went inside." I thought back to Alicia and what she had to say. I needed to tell Colton now but I kept fibbing through the conversation. "Alicia happened to be there, so we decided to have coffee together and grab a bite to eat."

Colton refused to turn and look at me. His focus was still on our daughter playing. "What did you two ladies talk about?"

"Work stuff," I replied. I grabbed a chair and pulled up next to my husband. "Here's your coffee."

"You mean; you actually went to get coffee?"

I showed him my cup, which was mostly empty. "Did you think I was going out for another reason?"

Colton stood up and pulled a piece of paper from his pocket. "I thought you were running to tell her all about the list you found."

Before I could lie, I saw black circles on the back of the page. I knew in that instant he had dusted for prints, the one trick I overlooked.

"I can't believe you did this," I told him.

"And I can't believe you went snooping in my safe just to find your next lead." He sat back down in the chair and kept his focus on the yard. "What did you and Alicia figure out?"

His question took me by surprise. He wasn't mean or angry. It was more probing as if he knew I would pry into his investigation and turn up something useful.

"What do I get for anything I give up to you?"

Colton's head snapped towards me. "You don't get arrested for impeding an ongoing investigation."

I stared into his eyes. "You won't arrest me." I was willing to call his bluff. "You won't do that to Izzy." I took a sip from my coffee waiting for Colton to respond. He sat there speechless. "If you want me to tell you anything, then you need to let me in. We work together on this case."

"You know I can't do that."

"Don't fling that manure in my direction. We both know you can cover your butt by listing me as a consultant on the case."

"You have no experience qualifying you to be one."

I let out a chuckle. "And yet, I've been able to provide more information about this case than you turned up."

I could feel the heat coming from Colton's eyes. "Fine, tell me what you know."

I took a victory sip of my espresso as I settled back into my chair to feel more comfortable. "This list showed all the bars and clubs Shareem and her friends visited in the last month."

"Thanks for telling me something I already knew."

"Did you know one of the locations happened to be one where a woman was killed that same night?"

Colton snatched the paper from my hands. "Which one?"

I pointed to the Crowe's Nest. "You had Shareem listed there last week. It was the same night Drinna Adams was found dead after her shift."

"You think the two are related?"

"I'm not saying it for sure, but there's a good chance the killer thought Shareem saw something and tried to silence her before she had the chance to go to the cops." Colton jumped up from the chair. "Where are you going?"

"I need to get to work on this right away. If you're right, then Shareem is in even more danger than we thought."

"What about me? What about our deal?"

He rushed over and gave me a peck on the cheek. "I'll let you know if I find anything linking them."

There he goes, our superhero, off to save the world again.

19

C**hapter 19**
My afternoon was very low-key compared to last night and this morning. It was spent watching movies at home with Izzy and playing with her dolls. My mother went home for a few hours before returning that night. She had previously agreed to watch my daughter, since Colton and I were supposed to attend my station's Halloween party.

Where the heck is he?

I knew he was out chasing the lead I gave him earlier, but it was eight o'clock on a Saturday and there was no sign of my husband. I tried his cell three times; each had gone straight to voicemail.

"Hey, it's me. I'm checking to see if you're on your way home or if you're still working. We have the Halloween party. Call me."

Concern continued to grow inside of me with each attempt to connect. The doorbell rang the moment I hung up, signaling my mother's arrival. Time was up; I had to trust Colton was okay and he was still working the investigation. It was just difficult to go to a party, thinking something bad could have happened to my husband.

My mother's head bobbed up and down as she reviewed my attire, seeing I had been wearing the same clothes from earlier. "What's going on? Why aren't you dressed?"

"Colton isn't back yet."

"Where did he go *this* time?"

"He rushed off for a case." I glanced back to ensure Izzy wasn't listening to us. "I'm a little worried."

"Why? Do you think he's out with another woman?"

"No, of course not?"

"Did you check the station to see if he was there?"

Why didn't I think to do that?

"No, I only tried his cell."

"Then, he's probably fixated on the case and forgot the time. You should give them a ring while you go get ready for your party."

"You're probably right."

I left Izzy with my mother while I ran upstairs to get dressed. I decided to wear a costume to fit my after-work activities. I retrieved the outfit from my closet. I pulled out a large, orange sweater with matching thigh-high stockings. Then, I grabbed the short, red skirt and matching pumps.

Colton would have died to see me in this.

I pulled on the costume and proceeded to place a pair of thick glasses on my face, removing the lenses, so they didn't interfere with my contacts. Finally, I tied my blonde hair up and pinned it to my head, allowing me to place a brown wig over it.

Jinkies, I look just like Velma.

The reflection staring back at me was uncanny. I had transformed myself into an iconic character from a cartoon detective show. I couldn't wait to show Colton but he still had not returned my calls. I decided to try one more time.

I dialed the station, finding no answer at his desk. I called the main line, where the deputies had advised he ran out earlier to run down a lead on one of his cases. No one seemed to know where he had gone, but I was sure it had something to do with Shareem Kinsley's disappearance.

Please let him find her alive.

I walked downstairs and was met with a giggle from my daughter, along with some contained laughter from my mother.

"What's wrong?" I asked.

"This was not the costume I imagined you dressing up in for a Halloween party." Her face was turning red as she tried to restrain herself from bursting out with hysterics.

"What were you expecting?"

"Not this," she replied while waving her hand around to indicate my outfit. I didn't know if the comment meant I looked bad or just different.

"Is it okay?"

I could see my mother biting the inside of her lips. "Yes, of course," she quickly said with a smirk. She took another moment to compose herself before continuing. "Your costume just took me by surprise. I didn't even recognize you at first."

I guess that could work in my favor.

I sat in the living room for another hour waiting for Colton. I tried his cell two more times and left him a handful of text messages. I spent the time with Izzy and helped put her to bed. I enjoyed being a part of her nightly routine, and decided I wanted to take it over on the weekends.

By nine o'clock, I realized Colton wasn't going to make the party. I wanted to sit and wait longer, but I knew it would only drive me crazy. His voicemail would have been filled with my paranoid ramblings and tearful messages begging for him to call me back.

"You should just go," my mother finally told me. "He's a big boy and can take care of himself."

I couldn't let fear keep me from having a good night. Colton was armed and had a whole station of deputies ready to put their lives on the line for him if something were to happen.

"You're right," I replied. "If Colton gets home before I do, remind him we had the Halloween party tonight, and have him call me immediately."

"Can I beat him over the head with a frying pan for making you worry all night?"

The request was tempting but I wanted my husband in one piece. "No, I'll handle his punishment later."

I walked out to my car and drove it to Alicia's house. The door opened, revealing an A-line midi skirt paired with a white button-down blouse. Her dark brown hair had been hidden behind a short, blonde, curly wig.

"Look at you," I callout out from her driveway. "Someone has an Ethel look going on tonight. Makes me re-think my outfit."

Alicia let out a laugh. "That would have been perfect. I guess that would have made Colton your Ricky."

We both burst into hysterics at the thought of my husband dressed up in a fifties style suit, playing bongos, and singing Babalu. I entered Alicia's house and noticed her husband, Tim, sitting in a pair of dress pants, a white, button-down shirt, and a loosened tie. He had a bald cap on his head with buzzed hair around the sides and back.

"How are you doing, Fred?" I joked.

"Not too bad, Velma," he replied. "Where's your other half?"

The smile faded from my face while shrugging my shoulders. "He's working a case; chasing down leads; catching criminals."

"So, it's just the three of us tonight?"

"Yes, sir, but he may meet up with us later."

Tim slapped his hands on his lap as he rose up from the couch. "Should we get going then?"

Alicia and I agreed. I knew it would take us a while to arrive at the bar. It was already nine-thirty, and I wanted to enjoy the rest of my night out. Alicia and I already spent one night at a bar, but that was investigative work. Drinking was secondary to the case. But tonight, there was nothing stopping me from relaxing with my best friend.

We drove into Atlanta, to Vortex, where a large crowd had already gathered inside to party. More than a dozen of my co-workers and their dates were among them, each wearing a costume.

Roger was one of the first to say hello. He tried to play it cool at the station, but he made a beeline for me seconds after I walked through the door. It was almost as if he had been waiting for my arrival. He stood in front of me with two beers in his hand. One was held out as Roger asked if I wanted a drink.

I never accepted a drink from someone other than the bartender. It was the way I carried myself during my college years, and I continued following that rule to this day.

"No thank you," I replied. "I wanted to say hi to everyone first."

It was a complete lie, but I said it to be nice without making Roger feel like I was blowing him off. I continued walking around the bar, eventually greeting Emma, the morning show meteorologist, and her boyfriend. I waved hello to Ben and a few other reporters I recognized. Finally, I made it to the bar and signaled the woman behind it.

Roger appeared next to me moments later. "Here, I got you a beer."

"Thanks, but I was in the mood for something else." A bottle would have been easier for me to walk around with and not worry about anyone slipping something into my drink. If I ordered another beer, Roger would have been insulted. "Can I have a margarita?"

I could feel his eyes checking me out. "Velma, huh? I pictured you more to be more like Daphne."

That had become the theme of the night. Why did I choose the intellectual one, who hid behind sweaters and glasses, rather than dress like the more stylish member of the group? I was sure Roger was picturing me in the purple dress with a red wig, but I wasn't in the mood to be ogled by anyone other than my husband.

"I'm a much bigger fan of the woman who can observe a mystery, locate the clues and evidence, and solve a case before anyone else on the team while putting together a plan to catch the bad guy."

Roger nodded while I spoke. "That's an interesting take on her character." He tried so hard to make me believe he was interested in a meaningful conversation.

"What are your thoughts on Velma?"

"I viewed her as a brainy, know-it-all, who liked to show off. She had to prove she was better than everyone by solving the case while her team felt clueless."

And that explains why I don't usually ask for Roger's opinion on pretty much anything.

Thankfully, the bartender brought my drink over, which made the perfect excuse for me to stop talking to Roger and make a break for Alicia. Unfortunately, he followed me.

"Where's your husband, tonight?"

That was another question I had to deal with from everyone I spoke to that night. It just felt more awkward being asked by a man whom I believed to be hitting on me.

"He is working on a case. He should be here later."

I finally saw an opening to slip through the crowd and distance myself from Roger. I located Alicia and Tim, sticking to their side for the remainder of the night. I explained the situation, and they in turn, kept me away from him.

I don't know why Roger had decided to pursue me. He obviously knew I was married. I always wore my ring. I talked about my husband and my daughter at work in a loving way. There weren't any signals I could think of being sent in his direction to make him think I would be interested in him.

We spent hours mingling with co-workers, drinking much more than I had the night before, and avoiding any discussions about the job. Colton never showed up. He left me there by myself. There were no missed calls or text messages apologizing for bailing on our night out together.

"He probably just didn't want to deal with everyone asking him questions about his job or any active cases." Alicia tried to come up with reasons for my husband's absence, but nothing she said could make me feel better about being ditched.

"He better have a better reason than that," I replied. I was already done for the night. "I'm ready to head home."

"Okay, give me a minute and we'll bring you back to your house." Alicia chugged her beer, something I was sure she would regret the next day. She placed it on a nearby table and walked me out to the cool, brisk, night air.

Tim's car was across the street. He kept his drinks to soda and water the entire time. I took the lead, wanting to go home more than the others. My foot barely touched the road when I heard a roaring engine. I glanced to my left. Bright lights beamed from a car speeding in my direction. My body was frozen in fear. I couldn't move. There wasn't enough time for me to snap out of it and dodge the vehicle.

Fingers pulled my sweatshirt as an arm wrapped around my waist. I was yanked back just in time. The car missed me by mere seconds. Alicia and Tim had broken my fall. I owed them both my life.

"That idiot almost killed you," Tim said.

Alicia and I stared blankly at each other as if we had the same thought running through our heads.

Was that a drunk driver, or did someone just try to run me down?

20

Chapter 20

Colton's voice echoed through the night sky. It barked out commands as if he had been standing right next to me. I turned my head, searching for the owner of the voice, expecting to find my husband.

"What was the make and model of the car?"

"I-I don't know," Tim shouted into his phone. "It was dark, maybe black or navy blue."

"Coupe or sedan?" Colton's question was more like a frantic roar.

"What?"

"Was it a two door or four?"

"Four, I think." Tim was trying to answer Colton's questions in the same rapid style they were presented to him.

"Make and model," Colton snapped again.

"I don't know," Tim repeated. "It happened too fast, and I was busy trying to make sure your wife was okay."

I figured that statement would have caused Colton to stop and ask if I was okay. Instead, he continued to focus on the details of what occurred. I guess it was the cop in him trying to get as much information as he could.

"Do you know which way it went?"

"It drove down Moreland. I think it turned right onto Euclid."

Colton's voice boomed over the chaos, repeating the information. I was sure he was calling for a BOLO on the person who tried to run me down. He told dispatch of an erratic driver in the Atlanta area, who was driving on Moreland and now on Euclid. Colton was doing everything in his power to hunt down the person responsible for the night's dramatic turn of events.

"Keep her there," Colton commanded. "I'll be there in less than ten minutes." I could hear the siren blaring in the background. I was sure he was using it to get everyone out of his way as he sped towards our location, especially since we lived forty minutes from the bar.

I crawled to my feet, finally noticing the small crowd who had gathered around us. They probably thought I was a drunk causing a scene, bringing entertainment to their night. One of the men asked about the speeding car. I wasn't sure if he witnessed the incident or had been eavesdropping on Tim's phone call with my husband.

Colton's report to dispatch requesting a BOLO brought more company, this time in the form of a navy-blue squad car with their lights flashing. Two officers stepped out of their vehicle and approached us with judging expressions etched on their faces.

I was in no mood to be treated as if I caused the incident. I was a woman in her late thirties, who went out partying on the eve of Halloween. They probably thought I was drunk and stumbled into the street and my friends pulled me back just in time. Maybe part of that was true. I was quite intoxicated and didn't see anything except blinding headlights. If it hadn't been for Tim, I would have been blood splatter on the street outside of the bar and tomorrow morning's top story.

News reporter drunkenly stumbles into street and flattened by hit-and-run driver.

Tim walked up to the officers and gave his account of what happened. Unfortunately, without a plate number or car description, there wasn't much the police could have done for us.

Another car came to a screeching halt with the lights flashing and siren canceling all other sounds around us. Colton jumped out of the driver's seat and rushed to my side.

"Are you okay?"

"Yes, thanks to Tim and Alicia. They pulled me out of the way just as the car ran over the spot I had been standing on."

Colton pushed himself away, keeping me at arm's length as he looked into my eyes. "Did you see anything?"

I was getting tired of being asked that question. Everyone had good intentions, and they just wanted to catch the person who caused the incident. Colton had a different look in his eye as he posed the question. I could tell he wanted to track down the person to hurt them just like they had almost done to me.

"No," I replied. "I remember leaving the bar. I walked into the street. I heard an engine rev, and then there was a pair of lights. They blinded me from seeing anything else."

"They probably used their high-beams." Colton was turning into cop mode. "How far back did they start?"

"I don't know."

"Did they seem like they were out of control or gunning for you?"

"I don't know," I barked. "It happened so fast, and I had no time to get out of the way."

Colton nodded. "Did the police take your statement?" I shook my head no in reply. "Then, come with me. I want you to speak with them, so I can get you back home."

I felt like a kid being brought to the principal's office by their teacher. I almost expected Colton or the other officers to chastise me for what happened, as if it had been my fault. Maybe it was for not reacting quickly enough. Maybe if I hadn't been drinking, the driver might not have come as close to hitting me.

Colton stood by my side as I told the police everything I could re-member. I answered their questions, but I was unable to give them any useful information. Once we were done, Colton led me away from the officers and back towards Tim and Alicia.

"Are you guys okay to drive back on your own, or do you need a ride?" Colton asked.

"Tim hasn't had a single drink all night," Alicia advised.

Colton nodded, confirming he understood. "Perfect, but I will follow you back to your house, just to ensure you get home safe."

Alicia and I stared at each other with a look of concern etched on her face. I was sure I wore a similar expression. Colton was being overprotective, which increased my internal alert level.

Was someone after me?

Colton loaded the four of us into his car and drove us across the street, where Tim had been parked.

"I'll be right behind you," Colton advised.

Tim and Alicia exited our vehicle and timidly climbed into their own. They led the way back to their house, with Colton keeping a close distance.

I sat in silence for the first ten minutes, until the urge to speak became too great. I needed to question my husband, and I was afraid it would come off as a nagging wife.

"Where were you all night?" Yup, I heard it in my tone. It sounded accusatory and a bit needy.

"I was out following up on the leads *you* gave me." I had a feeling Colton was working the case, but I didn't expect him to admit it. "I started by visiting Crowe's Nest, and I managed to convince them to give me their security footage from the night Drinna Adams was murdered. Then, I went to Tavern and ran through their red tape to get the video from the night Shareem Kinsley went missing."

Colton had been very busy. It was no wonder why he refused to answer his cell and had not returned any of my calls or texts. Colton telling me what evidence he obtained confirmed his willingness to share information about the case. That was more than enough to excuse him standing me up. But now, I needed to confirm my theory of the two cases being connected.

"Did you find anything?"

"I've been at it for hours. We are still reviewing the footage to see if there was anything useful. I'll probably be at the station all day tomorrow combing through every frame until we find something."

"Are you still working my suggestion of the two cases being linked?"

Colton nodded. "That's what we're looking for. I need something to show how or why they would be connected, but nothing has proven your theory as of now."

I let out a deep sigh. "I'm sure you'll find the link." My mind began to wander off a bit, finding the next level to jump up to in my paranoid theory. "I wonder if the scream I heard the other night had something to do with Shareem's disappearance."

Colton turned his head towards me with a look of disbelief on his face. "Don't tell me you plan on pinning this on Mr. Alexander, too?"

"I'm sure you're right about him. I just can't help thinking about it. The scream came from his general direction. His wife has been missing for days, and he was there, at Tavern, when Alicia and I were there last night. Plus, the items he purchased the other day are incredibly suspicious."

"Serena, we already went through this." I heard the growl in his voice, warning me to back off.

"Yes, but he hasn't set up any decorations yet. And I was willing to back off until he threatened me at Tavern."

"You never told me that. What did he say?"

"He just told me to stay away or else I would be arrested, and some other comments about men needing to rescue me."

"Sounds to me like he was making sure you weren't following him."

"I wasn't," I replied. "I was only there to check to see if anyone recalled seeing Shareem there. Finding Mr. Alexander last night, made me question if he should stay on my list of suspects."

"You better leave that man alone."

I blew out a deep breath, finally ready to admit to recognizing other people at the bar last night as well.

"I saw a few more from our community at Tavern."

Colton's lips clenched at my statement. "So, now you want me to investigate more of our neighbors? You do realize Tavern is the closest bar to our area?"

"I know, but so is the coffee shop where I talked about the list with Alicia about the places Shareem had been."

"You discussed *that* in public?" His voice was no longer filled with playful annoyance. It was replaced with anger. "Anything else I should know about?"

I agreed it was a stupid move, but I needed to finish telling my husband everything I thought about the cases.

"Where do we go from here with the investigation?"

"Oh no," Colton replied. "You've had enough time playing detective. It's time you leave the rest to me."

I pushed my body to face Colton's. "You said we could work on this together. I am not about to let you rip this away from me again."

"Serena, you almost got hit by a car tonight."

"It was probably some idiot who had too much to drink."

We both knew it was a possibility, but I was sure Colton believed it to be an attempt on my life.

"You have been attacking this investigation hard and had been speaking to Shareem's friends and family. You went to the same bar she was last seen at. You started questioning people who worked there, and then talked about this in a public at a coffee shop. You could have inadvertently come across the person responsible, and now they are looking to shut you up, permanently."

It was possible Drinna's killer and Shareem's kidnapper overheard me at the bar or the coffee shop.

"Okay, I'll be more careful."

"No, you're going to stay away from the case all together."

"I can't; my station is expecting my story on Shareem Kinsley."

I really didn't think it was going to be missed had I decided to step away from the segment, but I owed it to Shareem's family and friends.

"We'll see how the station feels about it once they learn you were almost killed by the possible suspect."

I sat back in the passenger seat with my arms folded across my chest. I was not about to let Colton take away my story. I was close to the truth, and I needed to help bring the case to a close.

21

C<u>**hapter 21**</u>

C I slept-in for the second day in a row. Part of me felt bad. My mother was most likely downstairs taking care of Izzy again, while I slept off another night of drinking. This hangover felt worse than the previous one. Even looking at the blinds, holding back the rays of sunshine attempting to enter my bedroom, hurt my head. The searing pain reminded me of the idiot I had been the night before.

Thank God I'm alive.

That was the first thought that came to mind. The next was how lucky I was to have friends watching my back. I knew spending the day in bed would have been a waste of time. It was a slap in the face of the second chance I had been granted last night.

I pushed the blanket aside and crawled out of the bed. It took me several minutes to get my bearings, but I managed to get up and make it to the bathroom without hurling the remnants of my party night.

The bathroom mirror was the next reminder of how bad I felt. The short brown wig was clinging to my own blonde strands. I ripped it off and stared at the almost comical sight. The dark make-up around my eyes made it look like I had been beaten up. My lipstick had smeared a bit, which made it look like I had made out with a clown. I noticed the orange sweater in the mirror. It had been lying in a heap on the floor at the end of the bed along with the red heels. I had one stocking on and the other was missing. The red skirt seemed to be the only part of my costume I was still wearing.

I cleaned myself up, put on some comfy clothes, and made myself look presentable before heading downstairs. When I reached the bot-

151

tom step, I could smell food being made in the kitchen. I smiled, thinking my mom was ready to dote on me like she used to, but then I noticed the chef was a man.

"You cook?" I asked Colton as I took a seat at the table.

He glanced over his shoulder with a raised eyebrow. "Don't get used to it." He went back to the food on the stove.

"Oh, why not? I kind of like this picture." I smiled with an idea of how to enjoy it a little more. "I have an apron if you want." I scurried to the pantry and pulled out a punk, frilly number with flowers on it. "Here, this would look great on you."

"Okay, I'm done." Colton dusted off his hands and sat down at the table. "*This* is the reason I don't do this kind of stuff."

"Come on; you never cook. I had to bust your chops over it." I took the apron back to the pantry and returned it to the hook.

Colton dug into his food and shoveled it into his mouth. By the way he was acting, I swore he was rushing to get away from me.

"Well, now that you're up, I'm going to head back to the station."

"You're working on a Sunday?" It was a rare occurrence, but it wasn't like Colton hadn't done it before.

"I have a lot of video footage to review thanks to your theory."

I vaguely remember him mentioning he would be at the station today. I guess the alcohol blurred my memory.

"You're *actually* listening to me, for once?"

"I do when you *actually* make sense, and you use facts to back up your statements. Plus, our conversation last night made me look at things from a different perspective. There's a chance all three events are connected."

He finally listens to me.

I watched Colton shovel more food in his mouth just as I fixed my own plate. I sat down at the table with eggs and sausage. I took a bite, and nearly spit it out right away.

"Did you season the eggs?"

"With what?"

"Salt; pepper; anything?"

"Why?" He asked.

I didn't want to be rude or hurt his feelings. Colton tried to make breakfast for us but managed to succeed in making the toast and sausage links, which were frozen and had instructions. The eggs were in desperate need of seasoning.

"Next time, wake me and I'll handle the cooking."

Izzy tried hiding the smile on her face. She apparently agreed with my assessment of breakfast. Colton grimaced as he finished eating. He put the plate in the sink and kissed us goodbye before running out the door. I could tell he was determined to solve both cases by the end of the day.

"I tried to tell him, mommy."

I walked to the counter and grabbed the salt and pepper from the seasoning's rack. I used both to douse Izzy's and my plates. I sampled the updated version of Colton's meal and nodded.

"Much better," I said.

Izzy grinned and agreed.

I spent what was left of the morning sitting on the couch with my daughter watching princess movies. We had just finished the first one when I heard a car door slam shut. Curiosity filled my mind, causing me to dart from the couch to the window to see who was leaving or who had arrived.

Bethany!

Ms. Alexander stood in her driveway with the trunk of her car open. She was in the middle of retrieving a suitcase and a laptop bag from it. I had been ordered to stay away from Mr. Alexander and their house. Nothing had been said about speaking with Bethany from the street.

"Wait here, Izzy; I'm just going outside for a few minutes."

I opened the door and rushed outside. I couldn't believe my eyes. Bethany Alexander was alive and well, standing right outside her home. My nosy reporter instincts needed to find out where she had been and what had happened the other night.

"Bethany, hi," I called out.

"Hello," she replied. Her eyebrows were scrunched up and her lips pursed. I could tell she was annoyed by me coming to speak to her. "Is there something I can help you with?"

"No, I just hadn't seen you in a few days. I wanted to make sure everything was all right."

She blew out a deep breath. I believed to be a nuisance, but it seemed she just needed someone to vent about her job. "One of my clients called late Monday afternoon and told us they were leaving my company for one of our competitors. My boss had me drive to Nashville to talk them out of it. I spent the whole week working out of a hotel room to work on proposals and numbers. I had countless meetings with my clients. We just finalized a new deal last night over dinner."

"That sounds- draining," I told her.

"They are not the easiest people to deal with, but they do make my company a lot of money."

"Well, I'm glad you were able to retain your client. "I was at a loss for words. My original theory had been blown apart by Bethany's return home. It meant Mr. Alexander was indeed innocent.

But if it wasn't him, then who was it?

"Yes, well, I have been working non-stop for a week straight and have just enough time to enjoy what's left of my weekend before going back tomorrow morning."

"I'm sorry. I won't hold you up." I was about to excuse myself and head back home, but the front door to Bethany's home opened. Mr. Alexander must have seen me standing in his driveway and stormed out to pick a fight.

"You," he roared. "I'm calling the police. Your husband can't save you this time."

Bethany's head was on a swivel, glancing back and forth between me and her husband. "Can someone please tell me what's going on here?"

"Mr. Alexander, I came over to profusely apologize for my behavior the other day and for hurling those accusations at you. I was wrong."

"Obviously," he snapped.

"Can someone please explain what this is all about?" Bethany asked.

"It's a very long story, one I was completely at fault over." I really didn't want to go into detail about mistakenly stating Mr. Alexander had killed his wife and was trying to conceal the body. I definitely didn't want to tell her I broke into their backyard to investigate her disappearance. "I really am sorry, Mr. Alexander. You had every right to be mad. I just wanted you to know I will not bother you or your wife again."

His angry eyes continued to burn a hole through my body. It took his wife nudging him for his concentration to break. He looked over at Bethany. Her arms were folded across her chest. Her head tilted in my direction. I couldn't see her face, but I assumed her expression demanded Mr. Alexander accept my apology.

"It's fine, but I don't ever want to see you in my yard, uninvited, again." That was a promise I was willing to keep.

"You have my word."

I excused myself and walked back across the street. Once I was safely inside, I called Colton to let him know what happened, and to admit I was wrong.

"Hey, I don't really have time to talk right now," he stated.

"I just wanted to let you know Bethany Alexander just came home from her business trip."

"And how do you know that?"

"I saw her pull into the driveway, and then I went over there be a friendly neighbor."

"You mean; you went there to interrogate her?"

"I did not interrogate her," I replied.

"But you questioned her about her being gone for the last week?"

"I just wanted to know the truth."

"Serena, we talked about this. You were not to go anywhere near the Alexanders or their house."

"I wanted to know what happened and also to apologize for my behavior."

"So, you're admitting you were wrong about him?"

I closed my eyes and accepted defeat. "Yes, you were right."

"And-"

"And I was less right." I let out a chuckle knowing how much Colton wanted me to say the correct phrase. "Look, if anyone had been in my shoes, they would have thought the same thing."

"Serena, no one would have jumped to that conclusion but you."

"Alicia did," I argued.

"Probably because you talked her into it. That poor woman is always ready to be your sidekick. One day, you're going to get her or you into serious trouble."

"You worry too much," I told him.

"And you don't worry enough."

I decided to shrug off his last comment and change topics. "When are you coming home?"

"I have a lot to do, and we're about to head back to Vortex again to see the manager about getting any security footage from last night."

"Will you be home for trick-or-treating?"

"I'm going to do my best, but this case comes first."

I hated how he seemed to put work before his family, but this was one time where I completely understood it. He was a superhero racing against time to save the woman in danger. I just hoped he wasn't too late.

22

C**hapter 22**
It was time to put Mr. Alexander, and the allegations I made against him, in the past. I washed my hands of the investigation. It was Colton's job. He was spending countless hours working my theory until it was proven wrong. Secretly, I wanted to be right..

I had my orders; spend the day with Izzy and enjoy my time off with her. That wasn't a problem. It was Halloween. There was a bunch of things for us to do before the sky darkened, and we could freely go around the community trick-or-treating.

It took me some time to get my head in the right frame of mind, courtesy of my drunken night out. We searched the T.V. for a few shows or movies celebrating the holiday. For lunch, we went out for fast food, something we rarely had in the house. It was saved for special occasions.

We returned home around one and turned-on Izzy's favorite Halloween movie. It was the one with the three witches who tried to eat the kids and teenagers just to stay young. It didn't take her long to finish her kid's meal. Her focus was on the movie and cuddling with her mommy. I wrapped my arm around her. I didn't care about the movie or the food. I just enjoyed spending time with my daughter after a very stressful weekend.

The sound of the doorbell tore us away from the T.V. just as the end credits began to roll. I got up to answer the door, finding Alicia and her daughter, Kimmy, standing on the doorstep.

I looked them over and noticed neither of them were in their costumes. "How come you're not dressed up?"

"I figured the girls could get ready together.

Izzy jumped up from the couch at the sight of her best friend. She ran over to hug her. She then stood, staring at me while bouncing on the balls of her feet. Izzy must have heard what Alicia said and seemed to be excited over the idea.

"Go ahead," I told her.

"Come on, Kimmy," Izzy said. "Let's go up to my room."

The girls didn't hesitate a second longer. They raced up the stairs before I could say another word. Alicia crossed the entrance and walked over to the couch.

"So that explains Kimmy, but what about you?"

Alicia dropped her chin to her chest. "I wore the costume last night. Do I really need to get dressed up again?" I nodded. "Why can't I just go like this?"

"Because it's more fun to put on some ridiculous outfit, pretend to be someone else for a night, and embarrass your kids."

"Once a year is bad enough," she complained.

"Do it for Kimmy," I told her.

"She doesn't care if I get dressed up."

"Then, do it for me."

"I already did you a favor last night by saving you from being a hood ornament on someone's car."

My mind flashed back to last night. I stood in the street, staring down a pair of headlights, as a vehicle sped towards me. I was seconds from having my blood stain the road. I owed Tim and Alicia for saving me.

"Thank you again."

"You would have done the same for me." Alicia turned her head and glanced around the house. "Where is your knight in shining armor? I thought he would be here doting on you all day."

"He's back at the station, reviewing the surveillance footage from the night Drinna Smith was murdered, and the night Shareem Kinsley went missing."

"You told him your theory?"

"I didn't have much of a choice. He purposely left the list for me to find, hoping I would give him some ideas or answers."

"How do you know he did it on purpose?"

"I came back home and he showed me the paper after he had dusted it for my fingerprints. It forced me to come clean about snooping in his safe and what I figured out from the list."

"That's big; he never tells you anything about his cases. I guess he's taking you seriously for once."

I was on the couch thinking about sitting on the deck with Colton again. He waited until I was done with my shower to close the safe door, which meant he was desperate for my help. He wanted it without having to ask. I wondered if he needed my assistance again. My mind was about to wander off into forbidden territory when my cell began to ring. I glanced down at the screen and saw Colton's name displayed.

"Speak of the devil," I answered.

"Huh…wait…what are you going on about?"

"Alicia and I were just talking about you being Peachtree City's white knight, saving and protecting everyone."

"Yeah, except my own wife," his guilty conscience replied.

"You shouldn't beat yourself up over it."

"I should have been there to protect you."

"Colton, you can't be everywhere at all times." I took a moment to let my words sink in, hoping to snap my husband out of his depressed state of mind. "Speaking of being places; when are you coming home?"

"I was actually hoping you could meet me at the station for a bit."

That was weird. Colton never asked me to go there unless I was in trouble for something. Maybe I was right in him wanting my help closing the investigations.

"What's the matter?"

"I went back to get the video from Vortex. I got the incident on camera, but it was really quick and blurry. I was hoping you could take a look to see if it jogged your memory about last night."

Sitting in a police station on Halloween was not my idea of a good time. However, I was interested to see the car who tried to end my life.

"I can have Alicia stay here with the girls until I get back." I didn't bother asking, but I knew she would agree.

"Okay, text me when you arrive. I'll come out to get you."

His last statement sent an uneasy feeling to the pit of my stomach. Colton continued making comments leading me to believe last night really *was* an attempt on my life.

"Go on," Alicia urged me. "I'll stay with the girls until you get back."

I put on my brave face and exited the house. The solitude of the car ride racked my body with nerves, wondering if the person from last night was going to come after me while I was driving. I kept using the rear-view mirror to check the backseat to ensure no one was there. It was the first time in my life where I felt pure fear, and I wasn't sure anyone was actually after me.

I pulled into the parking lot of the station and texted Colton the moment I turned off the car. He walked at a brisk pace and opened the driver's side door.

"Are you okay?" he asked.

I didn't want him to know I was scared. Colton was there to protect me; nothing bad could happen. I pushed the fear aside and tried to act like this was just a normal day.

"Of course; should we go inside?"

Colton rested his right hand on the small of my back as he led the way into the building. He was checking over his shoulders, reinforcing my belief that I was in danger. We walked to a room further from the entrance.

"Have a seat," he ordered. Colton was all business today. It was if a switch had been turned on, and he viewed me only as a witness instead of his wife. "Normally, I don't show the victim the video of the crime."

"Why?"

"It could be misconstrued as leading a witness, especially if you were to pick the suspect out of a lineup or called to testify against someone."

"Then, why are you doing it?"

"I need you to tell me everything you remember about last night. Don't leave anything out. I think maybe if you saw the video, it might help jog your memory."

I began with my arrival to the bar, and how my co-anchor wouldn't leave me alone all night. I didn't want to cause drama or to make Colton jealous, but he wanted to know everything. For all we knew; Roger could have been a killer; a kidnapper; or the person who tried to run me down just because I wouldn't accept a drink from him.

"Was there anyone else you recognized?"

"There were a lot of people from my station at the bar."

"How did they act towards you last night? Have you had any run-ins with them which would make you think they would want to hurt you?"

"No, we all get along. No one acted differently other than Jean."

"What happened with her?"

"She had a little too much to drink and she was getting too friendly with a couple of the guys from work and some other men at the bar too."

Colton shook his head in disbelief. "Serena, this is serious. I need you think back to last night. Was anyone watching you? Did anyone look suspicious?"

There wasn't much I could tell him. I wasn't paying attention to everyone around me. I didn't know I was supposed to be on high alert. I was too busy drinking and having a great night out with my friends.

"No," I finally said. I felt ashamed as if I let Colton down.

"Okay, let's play the video. Maybe that can help you."

He queued up the footage from outside the bar. There were only a few seconds showing a dark four-door speeding past the spot I had been standing. I saw Tim and Alicia pull me back just in time. They really had acted just in time. I think a second later, and I would have been dead.

"Can you roll it again?" I asked.

Colton rewound the video and let it play. I watched my near-death experience happen again, but it was going too fast for me to see anything.

"Can you try one more time; this time a little slower?"

Colton queued up the footage. This time, it showed frame by frame as the car entered the scope of the camera.

"Freeze it there."

Colton paused the video perfectly. The image of the car was a little blurry, but I was finally able to view it.

"Do you remember something?"

"No," I replied while getting up from the chair. I approached the screen and stared at the picture. "Were there any reports of an erratic driver after our call?"

"I've been checking, but there hasn't been anything matching the description of that car or any other incidents from last night."

That statement confirmed my fear. It was an attempt to shut me up. Maybe they meant to scare me off the case, but I was more determined to help put the person responsible behind bars.

"Have you checked any of the other surveillance footage from the other bars for a car to see if a car with a similar make and model had been there?"

Colton let out a chuckle. "I was so focused on the attempt on your life, that I hadn't considered checking the other security footage for the same vehicle."

Leave it to me to save the investigation again. I was happy to chalk my near-death experience as another win for me.

"Glad I could help."

Colton turned off the monitor. "It's going to take me some time to review the other videos, but I'll let you know what I find."

I placed my hand over my heart. "You actually plan to keep me in the loop about one of your precious cases?"

Colton tucked his chin as his shoulders rose and fell with a deep breath. "Look, I may have been able to connect the dots on my own, but you helped me do it a lot faster. For that, I owe you." He spun on his heel to look me in the eyes. "But don't think I'm going to do this with all of my cases. This is a one-time deal."

I put my hands in the air defensively. "Sure, whatever you say." I glanced up at the clock on the wall and noticed the time. "I need to get back to the house before it gets too late."

"I'll walk you out." Colton led the way back to my car and opened the door for me. It was an act of chivalry I had not seen from him since we first started dating, or maybe it was just him being overprotective of me. "Do you think Izzy will mind if I stay here and go over the videos?"

I hated how this case was making Colton sacrifice time with his family in order to put the suspect behind bars. At the same time, I knew it needed to be done. The person responsible had killed one woman, taken another captive, and tried to kill me too. I believed Colton viewed this as more than just another case. He needed to stop the suspect before someone else got hurt.

23

Chapter 23

  The sun began to set on our quiet small town. I had called Alicia from the road, advising I would be home soon. My anxiety pushed me to go a bit above the speed limit, shrinking my drive time. The girls met me at the door just as I pulled into the driveway. They looked beautiful in their princess outfits. Kimmy took the blue one with the blonde wig. Izzy wore a dark bluish-purple skirt with a boysenberry shawl and brown wig. I had asked my daughter why she chose to be the younger sister.

"Anna is special. She is smart, and brave, and willing to do everything to save her best friend/sister. She was able to do so much without needing powers."

Izzy was a lot like Anna, and she wanted to display their similarities in the form of a Halloween costume.

"Well, don't you both look beautiful?" I entered the house and moved towards the living room.

"Thanks, mommy." I watched Izzy look around as if she was searching for someone. "Where's daddy?" The look of disappointment on her face was obvious. "He isn't coming, is he?"

I bent down and took her by the hand. "Daddy is working a big case, in which a woman's life depends on him." It was a lot for a little girl to process, but Izzy knew her father was special.

She let out a sigh. "I understand. Hopefully, he saves her soon."

I glanced at Alicia. I was sure we shared the same concerned expression. "Me too," I replied.

The room was filled with silence. The kids didn't seem to know what to say, and there was nothing more I was able to share.

I reached for Izzy's Halloween bag and handed it to her. "Should we get going?"

"You're not getting dressed first?" Alicia asked. There was no way she was letting me off the hook after I forced her to don her costume from the night before.

It would have been fun to be Velma for another night, but that outfit was a wrinkled mess lying at the foot of my bed. I had another choice waiting for me, something easier to jump into quickly.

"Sure, I just need a few minutes."

I hurried up the stairs and changed out of my clothes. I opted for comfort and something that wouldn't be an attention getter. I grabbed a pair of black workout pants with red stripes going down the legs. They were just warm enough for the cool October night. I pulled my bold, red, Bulldogs sweatshirt to ensure I didn't catch a chill. I put a whistle around my neck and snatched a clipboard from my desk.

"Seriously," Alicia said when she saw me. "I dressed up like Ethel again, and you're dressed like you're about to curl up on the couch to watch a football game."

"I told you the other day I was going as a coach." I put the whistle in my mouth and blew on it to illustrate my point. "Okay team, here's our strategy for tonight." I bent down on one knee and motioned for the girls to get closer. "We're going to attack a lot of houses tonight. We're going to hit them hard. You're going to score a lot of candy. And no matter what happens, at the end of the night, you're all winners."

Izzy and Kimmy stared at me. They probably didn't know whether to laugh or cry from utter embarrassment.

"I think you proved your costume," Alicia said. "How about we start before the block is swarmed with kids?"

"Good thinking, Assistant Coach Ethel."

I let the girls walk out the door, accompanied by Alicia. I opened the closet door and grabbed a megaphone to take with us. I figured it was a great accessory for my costume, and it was another way to keep the girls close to us if they got too far ahead.

The four of us met in front of the house and began walking up and down the block. Almost every home had a bowl of candy sitting on a table with their owners sitting behind it. Some were dressed up, embracing the holiday. Others decided to participate by handing out treats in their plain clothes. It took us a half hour to return to our starting point. The next house sat across from mine.

I tapped Alicia on the shoulder. "I think you need to take the girls to the next one without me."

Alicia's eyes grew wide as she stared at the Alexander house. "Are you sure it's safe for us to go there?"

I could see how nervous Alicia was at the thought of going with the girls to the house owned by a man I accused of murder. I quickly realized I had not updated my best friend on the latest bit of information.

She has no idea Bethany is alive and back at the house.

"Someone has to go, and I made a promise to Colton I would never go near that house again."

Alicia marched up the walkway with Izzy and Kimmy at her side. Instead of ringing the doorbell, they followed the path around back.

I remained tight-lipped and did my best not to burst into laughter the moment they walked towards the house. She returned five minutes later with a petrified look on her face.

"Serena, you should have seen it back there." Alicia kept glancing over her shoulder as we moved onto the next house. "He turned his backyard into some kind of creepy cemetery."

I was trying very hard to stay in character and playing along with our previous theory of Mr. Alexander being a killer.

"What did it look like?" I was genuinely interested. Mr. Alexander supposedly loved Halloween and was putting on a display for the first time since we had moved to the neighborhood.

"It was dark. I couldn't really see anything. There were graves near the gate." Alicia turned towards me with her eyes nearly bulging out of her head. "Do you think his wife was buried in one of them?"

"I don't know. Maybe we should go back and find out."

"No," Alicia said. "Please, don't make me."

"Did he recognize you?"

"I don't think so."

"Then, you have to do it. He knows me. I'll be arrested on sight."

The four of us rounded the corner. The girls ran up to the next house while Alicia and I continued our conversation. I noticed she kept looking over her shoulder, almost expecting Mr. Alexander to come after us.

"So, I have a confession to make." I couldn't hold it back any longer. I had to tell Alicia the truth. "His wife came home this morning."

Alicia pulled on my arm until I faced her. The fear in her eyes was replaced by relief and anger. "You waited all this time to tell me? I walked to the back of that man's house, thinking he was a murderer and that he was going to kill me."

"Truthfully, I ruled him out as a suspect last night before we went to the party. Seeing Bethany come home today just confirmed it."

Alicia took deep breaths as she faced a new reality, one where Mr. Alexander was not a killer. "Colton managed to convince you it was all in your head?"

"I know what I heard the other night. The scream was real." I considered the possibility of Colton being right, that it was a neighbor's T.V. being too loud. I still maintained the theory the cry for help had some sort of connection to his cases. "Hey, at least it helped Colton with his cases. Right now, we're sure Drinna Smith, Shareem Kinsley, and the incident at Vortex is all connected."

Alicia stopped me again. This time, she had a look of concern etched on her face. "You think what happened last night was on purpose? Do you think someone was trying to kill you?"

I didn't want to worry her. "It's possible the killer knew I was getting too close and tried to shut me up before I figure out the truth."

"And Colton is letting you walk around...at night...alone?"

"Well, I'm not *really* alone. I have you and the girls to keep me company." I noticed the look of fear return. Alicia was scared of what could happen to all of us, especially me. "Don't worry; nothing is going to happen here."

"You realize this is the perfect time for a killer to come after you? This is just like every bad horror movie. Kids are running all over the street. Parents are watching their children or busy handing out candy. No one is paying attention to the other adults walking around. Someone in a costume could easily come up from behind, stab you with a knife, and leave you for dead without anyone seeing their face."

"Thank you for that morbid assessment of what could be the end of my life." I know she was trying to give me a word of warning, but there was nothing for us to worry about. "This is a very safe neighborhood."

"How can you say that? You just accused the man across the street from you of killing his wife."

I shrugged off the question and continued following the girls. We rounded the corner and realized we had gone towards the dead end. Normally, I would have turned around and started to walk back, but my curiosity begged me to take a quick look over the rail.

"What are you doing?" Alicia asked.

"I just wanted to see what's down there."

Everyone in our community knew it was a steep hill leading to the woods. Kids occasionally ventured down there to play, despite warnings not to go down there. I attended HOA meetings where other residents requested the area be filled in, hoping to deter their children. There had yet to be an official decision made.

I glanced over the side and saw a shadow. I reached for my cell and turned on the flashlight. "I think someone is down there."

Alicia stood several feet away with her hands on her hips, staring at me in disbelief. "It's probably some teenagers hanging out. Leave them alone and let's go."

I moved a little closer. I had hoped the light would cause the person down there to stir. "No one is moving." I switched off the flashlight and used the camera. I zoomed-in to the max and snapped a picture. I increased the size on the image and saw a woman. "I-I think it's Shareem Kinsley."

Alicia ran to my side. "Are you serious? Let me see." She stared at the picture on my screen. "It looks like her. We need to call for help."

I wasn't sure if the woman at the bottom of the hill was dead or alive. We needed to act fast, and I didn't want the girls to see any of it.

"Take Izzy and Kimmy back to the house. I'll wait for police and an ambulance."

"That's not a good idea," Alicia replied. "Her abductor could be lurking around, waiting to attack you."

"All the more reason you and the girls should get back to the house." I knew my reply was not reassuring Alicia of my safety, but the person on the other side of the rail needed our help. Standing around debating what to do was only going to waste time we didn't have. "Please, take the girls to the house and stay there until I get back."

I called the local number for an ambulance and had them radio for police as well. It was difficult to express the urgency without sounding like a woman freaked out on Halloween night.

"Mommy, what's wrong?" Izzy asked.

I bent down and had to explain why her night was coming to an abrupt end. "The woman daddy has been searching for is hurt and needs my help. I need you to go with Kimmy and her mom back to the house."

"What about you?"

"I'll be back before you know it."

Her eyes were filled with tears. I couldn't tell if they were for the woman who needed help or if my daughter was just scared.

"Be careful," she replied as she lunged to give me a hug. Alicia tore her away from me as we heard sirens in the distance.

Time was working against us. There was a lifeless body at the bottom or the hill, believed to be Shareem Kinsley. Whoever it was, they were in dire need of my help.

24

Chapter 24

The sirens were heard from miles away. I listened closely, internally marking how far they were, and how many minutes until they arrived. Medics were first on the scene.

"Where is the victim?"

I used the flashlight on my phone to show the body at the foot of the hill. Then, I scrolled to the picture I took so they could see the position of the woman's body.

"Do you know how long she's been down there?"

"No, I just found her a few minutes ago."

The medics pushed me aside and began working on a solution to get down the hill and bring the body back up without moving it too much. They were moving fast. I guess that's what happens when a person who had been missing for a week magically shows up in need of medical assistance.

A few minutes later, three squad cars pulled up to the dead end and began to help out. One of the officers pulled me aside to ask me some questions. Before he could speak his first sentence, I heard one of the medics call up.

"There's no pulse."

My heart sunk into the pit of my stomach. Hope of finding her on time evaporated like water in the desert.

Was her voice the one I heard last week?

I glanced back at the community and imagined the walk back to my house. We were only a few blocks away, four at the most. It was possible the scream I heard last Monday was Shareem Kinsley calling

173

out for help. The dates matched up, which meant she had been down there for almost a week.

A lingering question burned in my mind. It was the same one I had been asking myself all week. *How did no one else hear her?*

"Can you tell me what happened?" An officer asked.

I recited the story of Alicia and I reaching the dead end with our daughters. I let the officer know I sent them back to my house to ensure the girls didn't see what happened. I gave him my address and the rest of my statement.

"Thank you. I'll send an officer over there now to speak with her. Do you want a ride back to your home?"

I should have taken the offer. "No thank you. I want to walk and clear my mind a bit. This-" I waved my hand in the air as if I created an imaginary bubble to encase the situation I witnessed. "It's a bit much to take in."

"Okay, be careful and stay close by in case we have any questions."

"I know the deal. My husband is the sheriff."

"Sheriff Colton Davidson is your husband?"

I nodded. "Yes, and I'm surprised he's not here. He has been working hard to locate Shareem for the last week."

"I saw him at the station earlier. I'm sure he just didn't hear the call."

"I'll message him on the way home." I ventured off on my own, trapped in my own thoughts.

In all my years of reporting, I had never been the one to stumble onto a crime scene before police. It had always been sectioned off with the press kept at arm's length from the seeing anything serious. I hated to be the one to find the poor girl lying there, helpless and dying while the world carried on around her.

I grabbed my cell and dialed Colton's number. It went to voicemail after a few rings. "Hey, give me a call when you get this message. We found Shareem Kinsley's body. She died in a ditch a few blocks from our house."

I kept walking back towards the house and inadvertently took the block before mine. It took me a while to figure out I was on the wrong street. I was about to turn around and go back, but something familiar caught my eye.

My mind flashed back to earlier in the day. Colton had paused the video on an image of the car who tried to run me down last night. It was sitting in the driveway of a house a block and a half away from where Shareem's body had been discovered.

This isn't a coincidence.

I approached with caution and slipped out my cell again. I took pictures of the vehicle and the license plate. I had the house number in my sight. I texted everything over to Colton's phone before placing another call. I received his voicemail again.

"Pick up," I growled. "I might have found the killer's house. I just texted you pictures of the car that may have tried to mow me down last night. It is parked in the driveway of a house not far from where Shareem was found."

I knew my next move was stupid. I should have gone back to the dead end and grabbed an officer to help or waited for Colton to call me back. I just couldn't live with myself if another woman was trapped inside the lair of a psychopath. I was the only person who could help in that moment, and I wasn't about to let another person die.

Ignoring all rational thinking, I walked up to the front door and peered through the window, searching for a woman or any sign of struggle.

It's too dark in there. I can't see anything.

I took a step back and saw the reflection of a man in the glass. I immediately knew, I was staring at the man responsible for two murders. My mind raced to the night I went to Tavern. I remembered seeing the same man in the crowd. He sat a couple tables to the left of Mr. Alexander. He also stood at the counter a few feet from where I told Alicia about Shareem and Drinna's incidents being connected. This man, whoever he was, knew I was about to crack the case. His desperation to hide the truth sent him to stalk me until he chose the moment to strike. He failed, but the look in his eyes, in that moment, told me he wasn't about to let it happen again.

I looked to the street, thinking it was my best option. The killer stood in my way. I couldn't tell how fast he was or how much stronger he was than me. My eyes darted to the open side gate. It was my best chance to run for it, but I had no idea what I would face on the other side.

Okay, Serena; good luck.

I spun on my heel and jumped over the rail to the gate. The suspect was already sprinting in my direction. I made sure to slam the wooden barrier just in time, causing a momentary gap between us. He ripped it open with ease and continued towards me. His backyard had been fenced in. I had nowhere to go other than over the wall.

I began to climb, hoisting myself up onto the wooden pieces. My leg lifted to swing over the top, only to feel a hand close around my ankle. My body dropped to the ground. I was sure a bone had broken upon collision. It would have been a small price to pay if I managed to escape the clutches of a madman.

"You shouldn't have poked your nose where it didn't belong," the man said. His face had been so familiar, but I had no idea who he was.

I saw him reach into his belt and he pulled out a knife. I had seconds to react. I gripped the megaphone and toggled the button. A loud siren erupted from the speaker, as if a cop car had just pulled up. The suspect glanced around nervously. It was the distraction I needed. I held onto the megaphone tightly and swung with my left hand. It smashed against the side of his head, freeing me to continue climbing towards safety.

I landed in another yard. Fog had covered the ground, causing me to stumble as I tried to escape. I believed the suspect was only seconds behind me. He was surely in pursuit. The knife lunged at my head. The devastating blow should have ended my life. Instead, it connected with the megaphone.

That was twice you saved my life tonight.

I decided to stop playing defense and tried to go on the attack. I had taken a few self-defense courses and a little bit of kickboxing. I was confident enough to hold my own in a fight. But the moment I took a swing, my target blocked and threw me to the ground.

"I don't want to do it, but you leave me no choice." He picked up the knife and approached cautiously.

"You don't want to kill me, but you had no problem murdering two other innocent women?"

"You think I wanted to do that?" I could barely see the man in front of me, but I could tell he was not a stone-cold killer like I thought. "Drinna was the love of my life. I visited her at Crowe's Nest during every one of her shifts."

I tried to inch backwards. "So, what happened?"

"She thought it was creepy, and thought I was stalking her."

"You two never dated?"

"No, I had been trying to work up the nerve to ask her out. I finally tried, but she told me to leave the bar and never come back."

I don't know why he was confessing to me, but I was hoping it would be enough time for me to figure a way out of the mess, or to find something I could use to defend myself.

"Was that the night you killed her?"

"I didn't mean to do it. I messed with her car so she would be stranded at the bar. I figured I could show up and help her out. Maybe I could get in her good graces and it lead to a possible date."

"What went wrong?"

"Another guy from the bar showed up and ruined everything. He went to get his car, and I don't know; I snapped."

I could see he was getting closer to that same breaking point with me. I needed to keep his mind focused on other things.

"What happened with Shareem? Did you love her too?"

"No," he said sounding appalled by my remark. "She and I were friends. We spent Monday nights watching football together."

"So, why kill her?"

"Shareem knew too much. She had been helping me for weeks figure out what to say to Drinna. She was coaching me on asking out my dream girl."

"But once you killed Drinna, it was only a matter of time before Shareem thought you had something to do with her death."

"We hung out at Tavern last week. She told me about the girl from Crowe's Nest being murdered and asked if I had been there that night. We never lied to each other. I told her the truth."

I had crab walked into a small pile of dirt. My hands felt the cold soil beneath my fingers. "What happened next?"

She stormed out of the bar. I followed her. I begged her not to say anything. She promised it would be our secret, but I knew she was lying. Shareem turned to leave, and I took that moment to hit her in the back of the head. I brought her back to my place to talk some sense into her."

"I'm guessing she didn't respond well to being abducted."

"Don't say that. I didn't kidnap her. I just wanted to talk and she needed to listen."

"But she didn't," I continued.

"No, Shareem ran out of the house and down the block. She screamed for help, and I needed to shut her up before she woke up the neighbors. I chased her to the dead end. She climbed over the rail. I tried to warn her about it but she slipped and fell."

"Why didn't you go down there and check on her?" My voice was more aggressive and accusatory. I felt like Shareem could have been saved had he cared enough about his friend.

"She wasn't going to listen to me. I had to stop her from going to the police. I saw she hadn't moved and thought she was dead. I left her there, hoping she had died so I could get another chance." Then, he towered over me, clutching the knife in his hands. "And then, you came along and started digging into her disappearance. I knew you had to go too."

I was out of time. The killer was about to strike, and I had one last move left. I grabbed a handful of dirt and threw it in his eyes. It blinded him enough for me to scramble to my feet. The knife thrashed wildly in the air, keeping me in place. I tried to run but tripped over a stone.

Now, I was at the killer's mercy, and he was not about to spare my life. I was out of options, and out of time. There were no more tricks up my sleeve. He had wiped the dirt from his face and came at me one last time.

I closed my eyes, bracing myself for the impact of the knife to be driven through my body. I heard metal connect with something over my head, and then a thud hitting the ground next to me.

25

Chapter 25

I didn't know what to expect when I opened my eyes. I was certain death had been waiting for me. Its icy cold breath had caused me to shudder. When there was no accompanying pain, I wondered if I had died quickly. I wasn't prepared for the reality of what took place moments earlier.

I blinked and saw a man standing over me. His hands clutched an item tightly, as if he was ready to use the item to strike his foe again. But this man was different than the one who brandished the knife. He was taller, older, and wore an apron with blood splattered across it.

"You," I gasped as I recognized the man standing over me.

"I hate when people trespass on my property." Mr. Alexander placed the tip of the shovel on the ground and leaned on it.

I turned to my left and found my attacker lying next to me on the ground. His eyes were shut. I could hear him breathing, but I had no idea how long he would remain unconscious.

I scrambled away from the body, wanting to get far from the man who killed two women. "D-did you do that?"

Mr. Alexander offered his free hand to help me to my feet. "It seems you always seem to find yourself in a spot of trouble." He didn't sound like the angry man I had been accustomed to dealing with over the last week. "Luckily, you landed in my yard."

Mr. Alexander handed me the shovel as he walked a few feet to turn off a switch. The fog stopped spewing from the machine and slowly disappeared, allowing me to see the house I had tried to break into earlier in the week.

"I'm so sorry," I told him. My brain worked quickly to assess the situation and everything I had learned. My head turned towards Mr. Alexander's house, and then back towards the fence. "The scream-"

Everything finally added up. The woman I heard last week was Shareem Kinsley. I believed it came from Mr. Alexander's house because the man who lived behind him was chasing her.

"The police are on their way."

"We need to find something to restrain this man. He killed two women and tried to run me down last night with his car."

"I heard everything," Mr. Alexander replied. He pulled out two zip-ties and handed them to me. "Do you want to do the honors?"

I placed each around the suspect's wrists and secured the man's arms behind his back. He was no longer a threat to me or to anyone else.

"What happened?" I finally asked.

"I had just finished handing out the last of the candy and started to tidy up when I heard a siren coming from my backyard. I started to walk back and saw someone climbing over my fence. Then I saw another." He glanced at me with a stern look. "I called the police right away, thinking some punk kids were trying to steal some of my Halloween decorations. Then, I heard your voice and that man threatening you. I couldn't wait for the police to get here. So, I grabbed a shovel and swung as hard as I could."

"Thank you for saving my life." I glanced around the backyard, noticing the decorations that had created the creepy cemetery. "You picked the right year to finally decorate for Halloween."

"Tell that one to my wife. Maybe she'll let me celebrate more holidays, especially my favorite one."

We shared a brief moment of laughter just as the first squad car pulled up to the house. Bethany Alexander stormed out the backdoor, frantic about police storming the house.

"He's over there, officers," Mr. Alexander called out.

Police dragged the suspect out towards their waiting vehicles, allowing me one more viewing of the man who tried to kill me. I recognized him in passing. He lived in my community, but I had no idea who he was or what his name had been.

"Did you know him?" I asked.

Mr. Alexander nodded. "I think he rented the house in back of me sometime last year. He mostly kept to himself. I think we had one conversation the entire time he lived there."

His life was another mystery to unravel, something that needed to wait for a much later time. There was so much more that required my attention. I had police statements to give. I needed to get home to my daughter and hug her tightly. But first, I had to face the man who stomped towards me in the middle of Mr. Alexander's backyard.

"Colton, I can explain."

Before I could say another word, he wrapped his arms around me, pulling me into a loving embrace.

"I was so worried about you."

"I tried to call and text you. I found the man who tried to run me down. I figured out he was the one who killed Drinna and Shareem."

"I know; I got your messages. I jumped in the car and sped back from the station as soon as I saw them."

"Why didn't you call me?" I asked.

Colton let out a light-hearted chuckle. "I knew you were probably investigating on your own. If I called, it might have alerted the suspect and given you away. I called all available units to the address you gave me." He pulled away and looked at the man standing a few feet away. "Then, we got the call from Mr. Alexander, telling us there was an attempted murder in his backyard."

I pulled Colton towards me again. "Well, what took you so long?"

"I found the car in one of the videos. I managed to get the make and model from security footage from Crowe's Nest. The suspect was there multiple times a week."

"I know; he was in love with Drinna."

Colton stopped and stared at me. "How did you know that?"

"He confessed everything to me right before Mr. Alexander knocked him out with a shovel." I had everything the police and the D.A. needed to put the suspect away for the rest of his life.

"We're lucky he bought all those supplies for his Halloween graveyard." We looked around and let out an uncomfortable laugh, knowing I had accused our neighbor of being a murderer. "What else did you learn?"

"I should leave investigating crime scenes to the police."

"I don't know; you did a pretty good job on your own." Colton led me out of the backyard. "I think you'd make a fine detective one day."

"I managed to solve the case before you did."

"And you almost died, twice, while doing it."

I stopped and stared at him. "Does this mean I can help you on more of your cases?"

"No, you are not allowed to go near them ever again."

We'll see about that!

26

S ugar and Spice
Pumpkin Pie
Ingredients

- 1 Can Pumpkin Puree
- 1 Can Condensed Milk
- 2 Eggs
- 1 tsp Cinnamon
- ½ tsp Nutmeg
- ½ tsp Salt
- 1 Unbaked Pie Crust
- 1 Box of Pillsbury Pie Crusts

Directions

1. Preheat oven to 425
2. Combine puree, condensed milk, eggs, cinnamon, nutmeg, and salt into a bowl and whisk thoroughly.
3. Pour contents into pie crust.
4. Cut the Pillsbury pie crusts into strips and create a lattice or fun design, and place it on top of the pie.
5. Bake for 15 mins.
6. Reduce oven temperature to 350 and bake for another 45 minutes.

Apple Cider Cocktail

<u>Ingredients</u>

- 1 ½ cups Apple Cider
- 3 shots of Bourbon (I like mine a bit stronger)
- 1 tbs Sweet Vermouth (not necessary but tastes better with it)
- 1 tbs Lemon Juice

27

B<u>io</u>   Andrew Hess, the King of Cliffhangers, was born of Long Island, New York. His love of writing was discovered while studying psychology at SUNY New Paltz. He grew up an avid reader of fellow mystery and suspense authors such as James Patterson and Edgar Alan Poe. He designed his writing to be a combination of the two authors and added plot twists to his stories.

The cliffhangers began with The Phoenix Blade series, a government conspiracy series, which introduced a group of 22-year-old vigilantes hired by the government to eliminate people who were guilty of heinous crimes. Hess continued the trend while venturing into the world of crime fiction penning the Detective Ryan Series and the Detective Thornton Series. Readers have been glued to both book sets demanding the next installment from the author.

Hess has a love for multiple genres and has demonstrated this by penning several books in romance, thrillers, and psychological fiction with books such as; Learning to Love, #1 Fan, Finding Strength, The Kritana Contract, Trapped Inside: Living with Agoraphobia, and submissions in the Detours in our Destinations Anthology. He has also written two books of free-verse poetry with Chamber of Souls, and Hall of the Forgotten (an ode to Poe's Cask of Amontillado).

Hess won Indie Author Books Best Mystery Thriller Author (2015), and Indie Author Book Series of the year (2014) for The Phoenix Blade Series.

Hess was also nominated for Best Male Author, Best Mystery Suspense Author, Book of the Year, and Best Mystery Book (2015) for

Campus Killer by Wickedly Devine Divas, The Three Bookateers, and SNSBAH Promotions. He received several nominations in 2016 from Summer Indie Awards for Contemporary (#1 Fan), Crime (Conviction; Deadly Games), Mystery (Campus Killer; Scorned; and Conviction), Romance (#1 Fan) and Anthology (Detours in our Destinations).

With more than twenty books to his name, Hess is not done yet. He moved to Georgia with his wife and son to spend more time with them. The area has filled him with more inspiration to branch into other genres including horror, psychological thrillers, children's books, and mid-grade books. With so much already accomplished and much more to come, keep your eyes on this author as he takes you on a literary journey you will never forget.

28

Social Media Links

FB

https://www.facebook.com/TheRealPhoenix13/

Team Phoenix

https://www.facebook.com/groups/andrewsphoenixstreetteam/

Instagram

https://www.instagram.com/author_andrew_hess13/

Amazon

https://tinyurl.com/AuthorAndrewHess13

Website

https://tinyurl.com/KingofCliffhangers1

29

<u>Other Works by Andrew Hess</u>

<u>P</u>oetry
Chamber of Souls
Hall of the Forgotten
<u>The Phoenix Blade Series</u>
The Phoenix Blade: Project Justice
The Phoenix Blade: Awakening
The Phoenix Blade: Pandemonium
<u>Detective Ryan Series</u>
Campus Killer (Detective Ryan Series Book 1)
Scorned (Detective Ryan Series Book 2)
Conviction (Detective Ryan Series Book 3)
Frantic (Detective Ryan Series Book 4)
No Way Out (Detective Ryan Series Book 5)
Escape (Detective Ryan Series Book 6)
Atonement (Detective Ryan Series Book 7)
Truth and Lies (Detective Ryan Series Book 8)
<u>Detective Thornton Series</u>
Deadly Games (Detective Thornton Series Book 1)
Manhunt (Detective Thornton Series Book 2)
Deception (Detective Thornton Series Book 3)
Chaos (Detective Thornton Series Book 4)
<u>Sugar and Spice Mysteries</u>
A Scream in the Night (Book 1)
My Deadly Valentine (Book 2)

<u>Strength Hope and Love Series</u>
Finding Strength
#1 Fan
#1 Fan
#1 Fan: Obsession
<u>Stand Alone Books</u>
Trapped Inside: Living with Agoraphobia
Learning to Love
The Kritana Contract
<u>Mid-Grade Books</u>
Thornton Twins Detective Agency (Book 1)-Case of the Missing Purse